I0627113

Starting Over

on

Stoner's Mountain

Liminal Books

Starting Over on Stoner's Mountain is a work of fiction. Names, characters, places, and incidents are the product of the author's imagination or are used fictitiously. Any resemblance to actual events, locales, or persons, living or dead, is coincidental.

Liminal Books is an imprint of Between the Lines Publishing. The Liminal Books name and logo are trademarks of Between the Lines Publishing.

Copyright © 2025 by Heidi Sprouse

Cover Design: Morgan Bliadd

Between the Lines Publishing and its imprints supports the right to free expression and the value of copyright. The scanning, uploading, and distribution of this book without permission is a theft of the author's intellectual property. If you would like permission to use material from the book (other than for review purposes), please contact info@btwnthelines.com.

Between the Lines Publishing
1769 Lexington Ave N, Ste 286
Roseville MN 55113
btwnthelines.com

First Published: August 2025

ISBN: Paperback 978-1-965059-52-4

ISBN: Ebook 978-1-965059-53-1

The publisher is not responsible for websites (or their content) that are not owned by the publisher.

Starting Over

on

Stoner's Mountain

Heidi Sprouse

"You can't start a new chapter in your life if you keep re-reading the last one." — **Suzy Kassem**

Prologue

Jesse Collins rolled into the driveway of his childhood home and slammed on the brakes, screeching to a standstill. He hit the ground running, drawn, with a pull that was stronger than any magnet, to one light burning in the living room. The hair stood up on the back of his neck—there shouldn't be any lights on at two in the morning. Screaming—bloodcurdling screaming—shattered the night's silence, spilling into his brain. Loud thumping, something crashing, glass breaking only added to the chaos, the urgency thrumming in his veins. He sprinted up the walkway and burst through the front door.

The earth shifted under his feet and almost sent him to his knees.

His father stood with his face twisted in fury, hands wrapped around his mother's neck. Jesse barely registered her bloodied mouth and swollen eye, already black and purple. Her feet scrambled madly against the floor, her hands futilely grabbing at her husband's, her nails drawing blood, her face white. Lips turning blue. Eyes bulging.

Something inside of Jesse snapped, a crimson haze washing over his vision. He dove forward and yanked on her with unrestrained strength, pulling her free from her husband's grip. Coughing and gasping, she dropped to the floor in a heap, clearing a path. Jesse plowed into his father like a pile driver. "You are *never* going to hurt her again! So help me, God!"

Jesse's fists flailed with a will of their own, pummeling his father's face to a pulp. He literally saw red when his father's nose exploded with a crunch, blood splattering everywhere. Nothing satisfied him more than seeing his father's eyes swell shut. Anything so Jesse didn't have to look at the muddy-brown, bloodshot mess that had terrorized him all his life. He didn't notice the red and blue lights flashing on the wall. Didn't hear footsteps, the shouting, his father's wheezing. Didn't hear his own gasping turning into a sob as twenty-eight years of frustration finally boiled over. He grabbed what was left of the few gray tufts of his monster's hair and banged his head against the floor until someone muscled him back and slapped cuffs on his wrists. Only then did he hear his mother's soft crying through the open door of an ambulance as they hauled him past her.

An officer shielded his head, helping him duck into the back of a police cruiser. Jesse leaned forward, elbows digging into his knees, hands covering his face. Trying to blot out the vivid images of the last few minutes pounding in his head, breathing so hard, he was on the verge of hyperventilating, he fought to take in air. He barely noticed the officer's hand on his shoulder, standing beside the open door of the car after they pulled into the station. "Son, just breathe in. Now, breathe out. Again. Count to ten. Get your wits about you. When you're ready, we'll go inside. Get you sorted out." Minutes later, a strong hand gripped his arm and lifted him onto the sidewalk. A hushed voice murmured in his ear. "You just did what we've all wanted to do for years."

Jesse swallowed hard and sucked in a deep breath and nodded at the officer watching him closely. He took a few steps and dropped to his knees.

He lost everything he ate that day…and a stretch of days before.

Chapter One

Officer Cody Brown opened the door of the cell. Thank God no one else was in the small room except for the tall, broad-shouldered policeman who took up too much space on his own. Jesse already couldn't breathe. Put any more people in the cramped conditions and he'd smother. "Collins, the public defender is here to see you." He set his hand on his back. "Dylan Masterson is a good man. He's fair, and he'll hear you out. He's never hasty to cast judgement."

Jesse nodded. "Is there any chance I can use a real bathroom?" His stomach flip-flopped as it had—violently—all night long. Ever since he sat in the back of a cop car and relived beating the monster who called himself his father beyond recognition. Jesse didn't feel like turning himself inside out in the corner with nothing besides bars to block the view.

The officer's face softened. "Sure. Here you go. Just don't try and slip out the window, all right? I'll never hear the end of it." He winked. In a show of good faith, he stood outside, back pressed to the wall. "I'll be right here waiting."

Jesse closed the door, resisting the urge to lock it. He didn't want to send up any red flags, have them think he was making a break for it or ending it all. He knelt on the floor over the toilet waiting for his internal organs to make an appearance, the nausea intensifying. He swallowed hard. Breathed through his nose. Kept it down. He pulled himself off the floor and walked to the sink. He braced his hands on it and stared at his reflection. Face sharp from a few too many skipped meals. Skin whiter than the walls, especially pale against the navy-blue, jail-issued uniform. He caught fear in his cobalt eyes, deer-caught-in-the-headlights bright. He pushed the air out in a long hiss between his gritted teeth and sucked it in. Wet his hands to push back his jet-black hair. Thanked God for the umpteenth time his eyes and hair came from his mother. Because he didn't want any mark to be left on him by his so-called father. He couldn't do anything about the scars he hid under his clothes.

He straightened up. Set his shoulders. Stepped out.

The officer, someone he'd known since elementary school, was indescribably gentle walking him down the hallway, steadying him when his steps wavered. He opened the door to a small interrogation room. "I'll be right out here. You need anything or you want out, just say the word." He stepped in to whisper in his ear. "Everyone here is pulling for you."

Jesse sat down at a table across from a man getting lost in a dark suit. A stray thought worked its way through his muddled brain, *needs to eat better*. He took in faded brown hair streaked with gray, cut short. Neat. Proving he paid attention to detail. Crow's feet etched deeply, framing troubled brown eyes, more lines bracketing his mouth. Life, or his choice of careers, had worn him down. The attorney offered his hand in a surprisingly firm handshake. "I'm Dylan Masterson, the public defender. I've been assigned to your case. Would you please state your name?"

A lump formed in Jesse's throat. Almost as big as the boulder in the pit of his stomach. He cleared his throat and pushed the words past it. "Jesse Collins."

The lawyer nodded, glanced down at a file in his hands, grazed his lip with his index finger. He tapped his pen on the table, looked up and met his client's gaze head on. "Son, I know there's a history of domestic abuse in your household. I pulled up the 9-1-1 calls and arrests for your father. Quite a long list. I've got to ask you. What sent you over the edge today?"

The lump shifted, shooting a bitter taste to Jesse's mouth. *Don't you dare be sick right now, right here. Be plenty of time for that later.* He choked it down. Didn't look away. Didn't falter. "Sir, I've been headed here since the day I was born twenty-eight years ago."

The attorney cleared his throat, laced his fingers together. "Your father's alive. He's in rough shape and will be in the hospital for a while. He's pressing charges."

Jesse's hands gripped the edge of the table, a splinter digging into his finger. He welcomed the sharp stab of pain. "What about my mom?"

Masterson shook his head. "She's chosen not to press charges against your father. The damage *you* caused hasn't helped matters. When he came to, he insisted your mother got caught in the middle trying to stop you, that it wasn't his fault. Your mother says he's telling the truth and won't back down."

Jesse stood up fast, knocking his chair over, raking his hands through his hair. He paced from one wall to another like an animal trapped in a cage. Rage threatening to boil over. "She wouldn't. She's too afraid of retaliation—for good reason. Believe me. That's not what

I'm asking." He faced the attorney. Spoke very clearly, enunciating every word. "How *is* my mother?"

"She was treated and released. She's bruised, has cuts and abrasions. She's rattled. She came here first thing this morning and begged me to help you." The lawyer stood up and gathered his papers. "I'll do the best I can for you, son." He squeezed his shoulder. "If it was my mother, I would have done the same thing." He opened the door and stepped outside.

Officer Brown stepped in. "Anything you need?"

"I'd like my phone call." Cody set a cell phone in Jesse's hand and shut the door, leaving him in privacy. He punched the numbers his fingers knew by heart. Let the words spill the moment his mother picked up. "Mom, listen to me. I only have a few minutes. I want you to come to the jail. Get my debit card. My pin is 1995. Go to the ATM. Take out every penny. Pack a suitcase. Get away from here, as far and as fast as you can and don't look back. Call Aunt Helen or look up your best friend from college. Don't take your cell. Buy yourself a pay as you go. Use a fake name. Get out of Dodge. If you love me, I need you to do this for me. I need you to leave him. Now."

She sniffled, her voice trembling. "What about you? I've got to help you. I can't just leave you in jail."

"Don't worry about me. I can handle myself. The way you'll help me is if I know you are safe. You can't ever let him hurt you again. I'm not going to be able to protect you. Don't let what's happening to me right now be for nothing. Send a letter to me at the jail once you're safe and give me a way to keep in touch. Do you understand me? *Please,* Mom."

Soft crying drifted across the airwaves. "All right. I'll do it. I love you."

He leaned his head against the wall. Eyes closed. Heart hurting. "I love you more."

Her strained whisper squeezed his heart like a fist. "Thank you." Click. The line disconnected.

He let the wall hold him up. *Thank You, God. For helping me to protect her. To give her a second chance.*

His mother was a firm believer in second chances. She'd named her son in honor of Elvis Presley's stillborn twin brother. Small wonder. The King of Rock and Roll's music was the soundtrack of her life, a love she passed on to her boy. When he was a little, she held him on her lap and showed him a picture of her idol. "This is Elvis. He was amazing, but his twin, Jesse, didn't get a chance to show the world how special he could have been. I hope by naming you after him, you can shine a light for him."

A gentle hand rested on the nape of his neck. "I think you've had enough for one day. Time to get some rest." Officer Cody walked him back to his cell. "Good night. Call if you need anything. Anything at all."

That night Jesse's brain wouldn't let him sleep; replaying the events that happened in his childhood home over and over; bringing him back to a place he'd been trying to get away from ever since he was old enough to move out at eighteen ten years before. His head throbbed as the sunlight poked through the bars, stabbing his eyelids first thing the next morning. He sat up and pressed his palms to his face.

"Collins, I need you to come with me." A new officer, the one who sat with him in the back of the police cruiser, opened his cell door. "Your attorney is here."

Jesse stood up slowly, thoughts spinning out of control, making him question his sanity. "But I just saw him yesterday." Had he dreamed it?

The officer squeezed his shoulder. "The whole department pitched in to bring in the best defense lawyer money can buy. You did something we couldn't. The least we can do is help you get a fair deal."

"You can be anything you want to be, my little sweet pea." Mama rocked Stella back and forth as they sat on the glider on the porch and stared out at the yard, marveling at the sun rising in the sky. They tried to meet every morning with tea and hot chocolate, wrapped up in a blanket when it was cold even though the five-year-old didn't need anything but her mother's arms to keep her warm. Mama kissed the top of her head. "With a beautiful name from your papa, his love, and mine, you have everything you need."

Papa had been a firefighter. He may have lost the fight with a house fire last year, but he was a hero, saving everyone—four children, parents, grandmother, and family dog. He left his bold stamp, his big last name that was Scottish for battlefield, and his courage, in her and her mother, too.

Strong enough to face whatever life brought their way, just the two of them.

Stella turned and cupped her mother's face. "You want to know what I want to be, Mama?" It was a game the little girl and her mother played every day.

"What do you want to be, my little sweet pea?"

Stella pointed to the bird feeders in their fenced-in haven of a yard, bustling with activity. "I want to be a storyteller, filling the world with words as beautiful as those baby sparrows, free to fly anywhere my imagination takes me."

In answer, her mother sang to her and Stella echoed. Her mama nodded. "Oh, yes. A storyteller, you will be. Warming hearts and lifting spirits with every tale you spin. You can take your readers anywhere they want to go." She took her little girl's hand and pressed it to her chest,

"You'll touch people's hearts the way you touch mine."

Stella stood with both doors of a glass cabinet open wide, one hand pressed to her mouth, tears streaming from her eyes so hard, so fast, she could barely see. Staring at the note taped to a shelf where she couldn't possibly miss it.

My Precious Girl,

I have been in awe of you since the day I first held you in my arms. That was the day I became your everything and you became mine. I need you to know you were my purpose, my greatest gift. I am bursting with pride in everything you are and have become. You did it, Baby girl. You managed to touch people's hearts all around the world. I love you, all the way to the moon and the stars. And I'll be watching you, guiding your way home when it's time. Until then, keep shining, my Stella-girl.

Love,

Mama

"Oh, Mama." Her voice broke, her fingers trembling, trailing over shelf after shelf, jammed packed with books, thirty-two in all, by the world-famous, New York Times' best-selling author, Stella Blair. She didn't need to pull one off the shelf to flip the inside cover and see a personalized note. In every single one. Hand-delivered to her mother on the release day, by the author herself.

Stella closed the doors, wiped her eyes, and turned away. Not ready to box up the books. Or clothes. Or the photographs documenting the story of their life together from day one. Her phone beeped in her pocket, making that annoying sound; she never could figure out how to put on vibrate. She flipped it over. Hit the voicemail. Even though she knew what it would say.

"Stella, we need your final chapters *yesterday*! If you're going to do that radio show on Christmas Eve, you need to wrap it up. Have everything finalized in time. It's only two months away. Everyone's counting on you, and the publisher is hounding me. Please, Stell. I know this is a really tough time for you, but you really have to get to work again. Call me."

She set the phone down and walked away, through every room in the house where she grew up; through every memory they ever shared; through all the pain that nearly broke her the day she buried her mother—three months ago. She hadn't written a word since.

She'd come home to close the house, pack up, decide what to keep, what to give away, hoping maybe she'd find her inspiration again, only to become frozen, unable to move forward—

—trapped in yesterday.

In the end, the best money could buy got Jesse six months behind bars. Alone in a cell, waiting to see his therapist, someone he saw faithfully every day, sometimes twice a day. Sitting in dead silence, his stomach wound into a painful knot. Anxiety, his constant companion, rolling in a cresting wave that only grew by the day. Wondering. Where was his father? Because as long as his father was somewhere on the loose, his mother wasn't safe. One more day and he could finally find out—

—or not.

Jesse leaned forward, put his head in his hands, mulling over doing time in jail. He knew it was a good thing. He *needed* six months. If he was honest with himself, he needed at least six more. One hundred and eighty days weren't nearly enough to put out the slow burn that had been simmering beneath the surface since he was five years old. The first time his father hurt his mama. The first time his father laid his hands on Jesse when he went in swinging, tiny fists flying, crying and screaming, "Don't you hit my mama! Don't you dare!"

The flames had flared from time to time, sending him headfirst into a fist fight at school; pushing his foot all the way to the floor, speeding on the highway and mouthing off to the cop, getting a pocketful of tickets; losing his first job when he lost it and slammed his fist in his locker and dented it—at least he didn't hit his boss in the face; losing a string of jobs when his temper got the best of him. Everything boiled over that night he nearly beat his father to a pulp. He needed to get his fury under control before it became a raging wildfire that would consume everything good and decent inside of him, burning him down to ash. He'd come close to the point of no return with his father. He owed it to his mother to never cross that line where there'd be no coming back.

She wanted better for her son than the man who nearly destroyed her.

His counselor rapped the desk in front of him. "Nothing to say? Still water really does run deep. Just remember, you have to talk about this someday with someone or it will control you instead of letting you control it."

Jesse stood and offered his hand. "Thank you. For everything. The strategies you've given me and your advice. I think you've helped me more than you know. The one thing that worries me the most is what has my father been doing all this time?"

The counselor's eyebrows knit together. "You're leaving tomorrow, starting the next chapter of your life. You've got to stop re-reading the last one. Put yourself as far away from him as possible, literally and figuratively. He's not your concern. You need to think about you." He gripped Jesse's hand, giving it a firm shake. "If you need to talk, you have my number. Take care of yourself."

His therapist's words echoed in his mind as he walked down the corridor of the cell block, toward the exit. Every inmate offered him a hand through the bars, wishing him good luck. He was well-liked. He was quiet, listened to people. He didn't judge.

Jesse was in no position to judge anyone else.

As he stepped out into the light of day and filled his lungs, the nip in the air made him feel alive. He decided then and there to finish his therapy. On his own terms. Someplace where he could lose his past and himself—

—and never come back.

Chapter Two

Bare bones. That was the best way to describe the cabin. Minimal, rustic furniture. A woodstove in the corner of the main room that served as living room and kitchen with a table and two chairs flush against the wall under a window. The bedroom was snug, just big enough for the bed and a tall, narrow dresser, a small bathroom tucked in the back. No frills. No knickknacks. Plain and simple. It suited Jesse fine. Matched the way he felt.

Stripped down to nothing after half a year behind bars.

He didn't mind jail They gave him three squares. A roof over his head. His mother's screams didn't ring in his ears or pierce his brain. No more push and pull, the gnawing worry for her eating away at him any time he was away from home or alone in his bedroom down the hall while a hurricane crashed in his parents' room. The other inmates had left him alone. He wasn't sure why. If his reputation preceded him for what he did to his father or if something about him said hands off. No, this cabin wasn't much different from prison except for one thing.

14

For the first time in his twenty-eight years, he tasted freedom.

Freedom to go where he pleased, do what he pleased, say what he pleased, even if only to himself or the wildlife surrounding him. He no longer had to fear getting whacked up the side of his head, a black eye, or a fat lip from the man who was supposed to be his protector. His new home blessed him with the freedom to sleep, eat, get up or stay down. All his choices were his own. The aching in his gut, consumed by anxiety that today would be the day his father took his mother's life, finally let up.

He dropped his pack on the floor. It had to weigh close to a hundred pounds. He'd brought in everything he needed because there weren't any stores up here on the mountain where his grandfather lived as a hermit. He planned on following his ancestor's lead, staying away from town until there was no other choice. He would rough it. Make do or do without. He stretched his hands over his head, arched his back, and let out a groan. His muscles ached. Sitting in his cell, he'd had little opportunity to work his body, except for an hour or so a day in the gym, sharing equipment with a crowd, waiting for his turn more often than not. The three-mile hike to the cabin, the weight of the pack, the fresh air, and the giddiness of being out on his own, in a place of his own, set him to swaying. Light-headed, he sat down hard and fast, dropping like a sack of stones on the rocker by the fireplace. He closed his eyes, breathed in and out, finding his center. He opened his eyes and looked around. Yes. This would be perfect. His mother had kept her father's cabin hideaway a secret. Perhaps she'd hoped it would be her escape? Jesse didn't know about it until a package arrived at the jail, containing a map, a key, and a deed in his name.

Thanks, Mom.

He stood up and gave himself the grand tour: opened the closet, filled with blankets, bedding, and an extra pillow; checked the cabinets, stocked with non-perishables; peeked in the fridge and freezer, filled to the brim. A note on the counter brought him to a standstill, almost dropping him to his knees. "You grew up far too soon. You've always had my back. It's my turn to have yours. I'll love you always. More than you can know. Love, Mom."

He scraped a hand across his eyes and stepped into the bathroom to wash his face. A fresh towel hung on the rack. A toothbrush and toothpaste waited on the sink. Odds and ends filled the small shelf on the wall with matches, oil, and lamps. His mother had thought of everything he'd need to get a start in a place that belonged to one of his favorite people in the world, Grandpa Joe. It was more than enough. He couldn't ask or hope for more than the tiny hideaway on Stoner's Mountain, named after Revolutionary soldier, trail guide, and trapper Nick Stoner. Jesse hoped to take a page from the famous figure's book.

And learn how to re-invent himself as many times as it took to get it right.

He filled the stove with wood and tinder. Struck a match. Rubbed his hands and blew on them. In late September, a deep chill was already setting in. He sat back in the rocking recliner. Set himself into motion. Back and forth. Took out the picture of his mother she'd included in his package, tucked inside the pages of the deed. He traced his finger over her face, looking for a hint of the woman he knew. Her hip length hair had been transformed into a pixie cut, one that let him see her. No more hiding behind a curtain—a curtain that concealed the cuts and bruises, the terror. The dark color matching his had been exchanged for a blonde as pale as Marilyn Monroe's. Colored contacts transformed her deep blue eyes into a warm brown, staring out at the world from bright red glasses with pointed corners. She smiled. A real smile. Something he hadn't seen since childhood when his father went away for weeks, and they thought he'd never come back. She looked much younger and open—no longer shuttered. Happiness looked good on her. As far as the rest of the world was concerned, she was gone with the wind. He kissed his fingertip and pressed it to her lips, a stray tear splashing down.

"Good for you, Mom. Don't ever look back."

He sat by the fire, holding her picture, staring at the flames flickering through the open door of the wood stove until he couldn't stand it, couldn't sit still another moment. He stepped outside, found the stump and chopping block in the back, an ax, and a towering pile of wood. He brought the ax over his head in a great arch, swung down, breath spilling out in a *whoosh*. Every thwack was another punch to his father's face as each piece of wood split down the middle and fell to the ground, giving him immense satisfaction—

—best therapy a man could get.

Stella sat on the sofa in her childhood home, draining a bottle of wine. Staring at photographs scattered all around her. Of her mother and father with their new baby cuddled in their arms. Some of only her and her mother. Her mother took center stage in others. The story of Stella's life fanned out everywhere she looked. If only she could step into the pictures and stay forever.

The soft glow of the fireplace did little to thaw the ice running through her veins, nor could it stop her trembling. How could she feel so old, a husk of her former self, at only twenty-six years old? She tipped her head, threw back the last of the wine in her glass, and poured another glass. She wrapped her arms around herself. The phone rang. *For the fifteenth time.* Mother's answering machine picked up. "Stell. I *know* you're there. You have to talk to me! Re-join the land of the living. This isn't healthy for you. She's gone, but you're not. You need to get back to what you do best. Writing will help you to work your way out of this black hole of grief. Besides, you have a contract. If you break it, it could mean major ramifications. It could cost you more money than you know. You could lose your publisher. You've worked too hard for this to throw it away. *Please!* Stella Marie Blair, pick up this phone right now!"

Her best friend and agent, Angie Jackson, was fed up. Her tone said it all. Getting more agitated with every call. Switching to the landline when the cell kicked everything to voicemail.

Because the mobile phone was turned off.

Lose her publishing deal? Why didn't that scare her to death? Her mind carried her back to when she got her first deal. The exhilaration was enough to send her over the moon.

"Can I have more creamer please? Miss?" A little old man in the hole-in-the-wall diner called out, banging his spoon on the table.

A long sigh spilled out. Stella pushed her hair out of her eyes. "Yes sir, just a moment sir." She grabbed the creamer, topped off his coffee, and leaned against the counter, waiting for the next customer to walk through their door. She caught her reflection in the dirt-smeared windows. Bit her lip. Sorry, Mama. Guess I took a wrong turn somewhere.

The morning rush came and went, some regulars trickled in, pulled out her smile. Lifted her heart. Made that little bird of hope in her heart start singing again. Filling her head with ideas for a story. Always spinning around in her mind, waiting to be released. She grabbed her little notebook from her pocket and quickly jotted down a brief outline. She could flesh it out later. Alma, a sweetheart of an elderly woman who came every day like clockwork at four o'clock for her early bird special, nodded appreciatively. "Honey, you're lit up like a candle right now with those shining eyes and that bright smile of yours."

Stella patted her hand. "It's because I'm brimming with inspiration and just for those kind words, a piece of apple pie ala mode on the house." She delivered it with a wink. Hung up her apron and gave the next girl on shift a wave as she walked out the door, practically skipping to her beat-up old Chevy Malibu. She turned on the radio, full blast, rolled down the windows, drove into the setting sun...and sang along.

She pulled in the drive leading to a small cottage on the edge of a large estate. A wealthy widow owned the big house and rented it to her for a steal. With one condition: Stella had to pop in every day for a cup of tea and a bit of good cheer. Thank goodness because she didn't make much as a waitress. Her heart lifted to step inside her sweet, cozy little place. The kind of place she liked best away from everyone else. She hung up her apron, grabbed her notebook and pen, and headed out back to sit on the step. She waited for sunset. Closed her eyes and saw her home when she was little...when her father was still there with Mama...who gave her wings. How she wanted to live there for the rest of her days. She remembered what it felt like. Picked up her notebook. She started writing about her Forever Home, because no other place could replace the home in her heart. Even after so many years went by.

A river of words flowed onto the page.

One chapter. Two. The words poured out, poured out, faster and faster. She was up all night and kept hammering on the keys through her weekend off. One week later, she dropped her manuscript in the mail to an agent she picked by closing her eyes and setting her finger on her laptop screen. She didn't even think twice about it. She could feel it in her bones. Her story was good, right.

*This was **the** one.*

Two months later, she listened to her voicemail at work on her break. The agent offered her a contract and a chance to put Stella Blair on the map. She let out a whoop and spun in a circle, doing her best happy dance. The moment she got off her shift at almost midnight, she dialed the only number on her mind, wiping her eyes with a napkin from the diner as she waited for the rings. For the voice of her lifelong guidepost. "Baby girl? Is everything all right?"

Somehow, she kept it together long enough to talk. "I'm sorry. I couldn't wait. Mama, you won't believe this!"

But of course, she did. Every word. "I always knew you could fly, sweetheart. From the day they first put you in my arms."

Stella buried her face in her hands, shoulders shaking silently, lost in a memory so vivid she could walk into it. Until the phone interrupted her. *Again.* She yanked it out of the wall and threw it on the floor with an agonized scream. Drank another glass of wine. Picked up her laptop and scrolled down the list of Air BnB's in one of her mother's favorite places, the Adirondacks of upstate New York. She closed her eyes and tapped the touch screen with her index finger, mirroring the way she stumbled on to an agent. A remote cabin popped up, with no cell service, far from civilization—

—and the pain.

Yes. This will do. Her cell phone flashed. Even though the sound was off, she couldn't ignore how it lit up like a beacon. She hit the receive call button hard enough to make it spin on the table. *"What?"*

Her best friend stuttered on the other end. *"Finally!* I'm talking to you instead of a recording. I'm worried about you, honey. Let me come out there, help you through this."

Stella stared out at the pine tree in the backyard sparkling with white lights. One for each of her mother's fifty-eight years. She cleared her throat. "No. I need to be alone to work through this pain." *The unbearable hurting!* "I'll get the writing flow going again. I'm going to a cabin in the Adirondacks. There's no phone. Don't come looking for me. I'll be done on time. I've never missed a deadline. I won't start now. That would be letting my mother down. Trust me." The tears started again. She whispered, "Thanks for always being there for me, Angie, but I'm sorry. I need you to leave me be right now." She hit the end call. Filled her glass, emptying her second bottle.

She drank it down to the last drop and cried herself to sleep on the couch.

He stumbled from the bedroom to the bathroom in the dim light of dawn, creeping through the tattered shade on the window. *Damn roach motel isn't worth $50. They ought to be paying* him *to stay there. Still half asleep, he doused his face in cold water and clung to the edge of the sink. His head pounded from the rotgut whiskey he'd downed the night before to kill the pain. Ever since he'd taken a beating,* everything hurt, but his face worst of all.

He glared at his reflection in the mirror, bared his teeth in an ugly grin, poking his tongue in the gaps where three of his front teeth had gone missing. His nose had a hump in it that wasn't there before and was crooked. It whistled with every breath from a deviated…something or other…the doc called it. Said it could be fixed. *Yeah, right. Didn't even have a pot to piss in. Sure as hell wasn't paying for a hospital bill.* The collection bills were probably pouring out of the mailbox at his old place. Not his problem anymore. He'd been evicted and hadn't left a change of address.

Because he didn't have one.

The sunlight glanced off the jagged scar running from his temple down to his jaw, turning it crimson. Prodding at his cheekbone only made it throb. After so many months had gone by, it still throbbed, a permanent reminder of the bastard who ruined him. His fist shot out and slammed into the mirror, shattering it, blood dripping down his fingers, running down his arm, splattering all over the sink. He gritted his teeth, biting back a howl of rage, and wrapped a towel around his hand. One step closer to turning into a pillar of flame.

The room began to spin and his stomach rolled, bile burning its way up his windpipe, hitting the roof of his mouth before he dropped to his knees and threw up into the can. Puked his guts out until it hurt and dry heaves took over.

When he could peel himself off the disgusting linoleum, peeling and stained with sources he couldn't bear thinking about, he crawled back into bed. He picked up the pocketknife on the nightstand and carved another notch into the surface. Adding another mark to keep a tally of how many days he'd been living in filth. His only comfort? Planning his revenge. It would take much more than an eye for an eye. When the day of reckoning came, he'd take the scum of the earth apart, one piece at a time.

Getting through the day was like climbing a mountain—a mountain of rage, regret, and resentment, of lost opportunities, of the destruction of life as he knew it, if he ever really had a life at all. His mountain only grew higher and rockier, sending him on a harrowing journey up a slippery slope. *Every single day*. It didn't matter how much wood he chopped, how many hikes he took to the highest surrounding peaks, how much or how loud he screamed at the sky or the moon. His only consolation? His mother was on the other side of the country, safe, with a clean slate. He'd finally managed to save her from the monster who terrorized them far too long.

He stacked the wood outside his cabin first thing in the morning, like he had every morning since he arrived, lining it up against one wall, the stacks mounting to the roof. There had been one small, neat pile on the porch when he arrived. He stared down at his feet, hands on his hips, breath swirling in a cloud, drifting off into the distance. His heartbeat echoed in his head, his chopping coming to a halt. There was no more room for any wood. Not now. Not for at least a week. He grabbed the ax, swung it over his head, and lodged it in the chopping block with a growl. He *couldn't* be still.

He stomped inside, put a cast-iron kettle filled with water on the woodstove, and tapped his foot impatiently. He raked his hands through his hair, waiting for the water to bubble. He ignored his mother's humorous advice every time he waited for one of his favorite meals, macaroni and cheese, as a child. *A watched pot never boils.* He winced when he thought how fitting those words were considering the number of times his father tossed the pot, contents and all, against the wall, and sent him scurrying to his bed. Belly growling. Shaking. Tears streaming down his face. Sometimes with a fat lip or a new bruise on his face—

—or his mother's.

He growled again, struggling to control his rage, pacing until the water finally rolled, steam filling the room. He poured the scalding water into a metal basin with a generous squirt of cleanser. He plunged a sponge in, heedless of burning himself, and scrubbed the interior of the cabin top to bottom. Another daily task he set for himself. Only when his mission was accomplished, did he fix himself a cup of coffee. Strong and black. He cooked an egg in a cast-iron pan on the top of the woodstove, cooked a piece of toast the same way. He ate them both standing up. Looked in the cabinets. Nodded with a sharp jerk. End of his second week. Time to go to town. Another routine he'd established.

For some reason, he needed consistency in his life, now more than ever.

Two hours later, he completed the trek down the mountain and a winding road, past a few solitary homes, scattered far and wide, into the gone-in-a-blink town. Stoner's Hollow. With a gas station, a laundromat, a hardware store, a pizza place, a diner, and a general store. He stood on the opposite side of the road, eyeing the people walking in and out. Gathering his courage. Reminding himself, *he won't be here. Won't find you. Doesn't even know you're out of jail and doesn't care.* Jesse inhaled deeply. Shoulders set. Held his head high and approached the entrance. Like he had a right to because he did, damn it! He caught his reflection in the window before walking in, stumbled, did a double take. Jesse's mother wasn't the only one who had a makeover.

His father wouldn't know him if he walked right into him.

A beard covered his face, hiding his strong jaw, sharp chin, his mouth drawn in a thin line. His shaggy hair brushed against his collar and fell into his eyes, hiding them, too, exactly the way he wanted it. His jeans hung loose on his lean frame, any traces of fat melting off him while his biceps and chest muscles bulged from the hard work he put himself through day in and day out. He nodded his approval. Good. This was his fresh start too.

He stepped inside, the jingle of the bell over the door making him jerk, pumping the blood faster through his veins, heart beating loud enough he thought everyone could hear it. He'd become accustomed to the quiet of the cabin and the woods—preferred it—and couldn't wait to get back to it as fast as his feet could carry him there.

He scanned the store until his gaze focused on the woman at the register with a name tag, Sally Ambrose, owner of Ambrose's General Store. The older woman had a soft face and an easy smile, a rounded figure that made him think of a grandmother—something else lacking in his life. Light brown hair streaked with gray fell halfway down her back. Her warm eyes, a pale gray, lit up upon seeing him. "Mountain Man, good to see you." She was also the town's real estate agent who had shown him the way to the trailhead, shaking his hand, giving him a map, and welcoming him to her neck of the woods in case he needed any help settling into his new property. She placed the cordless phone on the counter in his hand before he even asked. "Take as long as you need."

He nodded, tried to pull out a smile but failed. "It's nice to see you as well. Thank you." He punched in the number he'd committed to memory. He didn't even have the slip of paper anymore. Just in case the man whose name he wouldn't let fall off his tongue ever showed up. Sally gestured to her small office behind the counter. He nodded, mouthing his thanks as she closed the door behind him. His heart rate kicked up, stomach knotted, waiting for the rings. Waiting for the only person who mattered to him to answer. She had a new name, new address with an old friend from the old days before his father was on the scene, in a quiet town the old man didn't know the name of on the other side of the country.

Sleeping with a gun under her bed.

"Hello?"

He could breathe again just at the sound of her voice. "Are you okay?" He *had* to check in.

A sniffle on the other end made his heart ache. "I'm good. What about you?"

"I'm all right. Make sure you take care of yourself." His voice went rough around the edges, a lump big enough to make him choke rising in his throat. "I love you."

"Love you more." Her whisper floated across the space between them before the line went dead.

He set the phone down, cleared his throat, blinked hard to clear his vision, and walked out of the office. He moved purposefully down the aisles, filling his basket as quickly as possible. Jesse *had* to get out before he suffocated. He didn't like to be seen or stay in town any longer than he had to. He laid his items on the counter, resisting the urge to tap his foot as the owner rang him up. He handed over the money as he read the amount on the screen. "Keep the change."

Sally snagged his sleeve before he could walk away. "There's a blizzard coming in. You can stay here, if you'd like, in the back room. I have a sofa bed just for times like these. My apartment is up above. I could bring you a hot meal." Her forehead creased, mouth turning down in a frown. "You look like you could use a good, hearty meal."

He pulled out his rusty manners. "Thank you, but I'll be all right, really. I've got to get back home." He thought otherwise when the flakes came down fast and furious, a couple inches an hour until he couldn't see through the sheet of white. The wind whipped around him, and the temperature plummeted. *In October!* His legs and lungs screamed on the trek up the mountain. And the anger flared, blazing hotter, threatening to consume him. He'd attended his therapy sessions without complaint; said everything he was supposed to say. Toed the line, but the fury still simmered beneath the surface, barely contained. On the verge of erupting. It wasn't a matter of *if* there would be an explosion.

It was *when*.

So, he chopped more wood in the middle of a snowstorm, fighting the howling wind and frigid temperatures. The exertion making him so hot he shed his coat, then his shirt, but not the anger—never the anger.

"Excuse me. Sorry. I am lost. Can you help me?"

He whipped around. A woman stood coated in snow, trembling, barely dressed for the elements. He met her gaze gleaming as bright as honey in a jar and couldn't move for an instant. He grabbed his shirt and shrugged into it, then his coat. Stared into wide eyes, taking up her whole face.

Lost? Weren't they all?

Stella parked at the trailhead. She skimmed through the booklet that arrived in the mail a few days before. Peered out the windshield, through the wipers beating to a rhythm that matched her heart. Gaped at the wall of snow coming down. She read the pamphlet again, questioning her sanity. *You'll need to hike in about two miles. Snowshoes are best in the winter.* It was late October. It wasn't supposed to snow for another month at least, except maybe a nuisance at worst, or Currier and Ives Christmas card pretty at best; an inch or two of fluff—

—not a blizzard.

She sat in the cozy nest of her car, heat blasting. Deliberating. She could stay here; wait it out; risk running out of gas with no cell to call and get rescued because she'd left it behind trying to prove she could pass the test of doing something out of her comfort zone. Even though she'd never gone camping for a day in her life. Or hiking. Or to the woods. She could turn around, go to that cute motel about ten miles away—*should* turn around—be sensible.

She stared at her eyes in the rearview mirror. Her mother's honey eyes, framed by the same golden-brown hair, reminding her yet again of the woman who raised her to be all she could be. "Or you can bite the bullet. Do this thing. Right now."

She nodded, zipped up her coat, pulled a knit cap over her hair, yanked on her hood, put on her gloves, tucked the keys in her purse and strapped it to her side. She got out, floundering in the foot-deep snow in boots that only came to her ankle. She shook her head, grumbling at herself for wearing boots meant for style instead of practical use.

She winced as snow crept inside, soaking her socks. She pulled on the handle of her suitcase on wheels, dragging it behind her. More snow filled her boots, making her shiver, and the wheels got hung up in the rocky terrain buried under the thick layer of fluff. She tugged on her suitcase, forging toward the trail. She scanned the sign: Stoner's Mountain, with a wooden plaque underneath stating, *Old Nick's Cabin. Two miles. Right fork.* Snow plopped down her neck. She bit her tongue to hold back a shriek. She nodded again and spoke fiercely to herself, "Suck it up, Buttercup." Her mother's favorite quote echoed in her mind. *A journey of a thousand miles begins with a single step.*

Even in high heeled boots with snow nipping at her toes.

Stella fought the urge to cry. The tears would probably freeze anyway. The wind stole the air from her lungs, cutting through a coat that felt like it was paper thin. It wasn't made for practicality either. She pulled out her booklet with the map, her hands shaking so hard she dropped it. She snatched it up and pinned her glove between her teeth. She'd peeled it off so she could fumble with the damp pages. The map told her to take the second fork to the right. A fist of fear tightened around her gut. She'd been walking *forever*. The snow was coming down so hard it was a whiteout. What if she had missed the turn? She glanced behind her. There was no sign of her tracks. and the snow was blowing. She wasn't sure she could find her way back down to the car.

You are going to freeze to death out here. The only person who knows where you are is the owner of Air BnB, and you've paid her for two months. No one will come looking until the animals have picked your bones clean. Quivers ran through her that had nothing to do with the extreme chill and everything to do with the gruesome image filling her head. She tucked the pamphlet back in her pocket, fought with the zipper, and moved forward. She stumbled for the umpteenth time, fell, and picked herself up again even though she wanted to tuck herself in a ball and cry.

Staying put is not going to get you anywhere, is it? Keep going, sweetheart. I have faith in you.

Her momma's voice pushed her forward. It might be a hallucination, but that familiar voice kept her moving toward a plume of smoke she could barely make out in the storm—*and* a cabin. She didn't know who it belonged to. *Didn't* care if it was sasquatch or the Abominable Snowman. She fought her way up the front steps and threw herself at the door, pounding and shouting. No one answered. *Someone has to be here. Where there's smoke, there's fire!* She went around back, stumbling again. She landed on her hands and knees. She lifted her head, wondering if she was delirious.

A bare-chested wall of a man stood at a chopping block with long dark hair and a thick beard, his breath forming a cloud around his head. Snow coated his body, evaporating almost as soon as it hit his bare skin, setting a fire deep down in her belly and making her toes curl. He looked like a character who could have walked out of the pages of one of her books. He split logs with an axe, taking a mighty swing with a grunt every time, in the middle of a raging blizzard. A pile of wood mounted on either side of him, climbing higher and higher. The snow, the wind, and his personal limits failed to slow him down. Stella grabbed a tree to pull herself to her feet, found her courage, and called out, "Excuse me. Sorry. I am lost. Can you help me?"

He froze for an instant before scrambling to shrug into his shirt and coat. A crimson tide rushed from his neck up to his cheeks. A bright blue gaze, hard as stone, swept over her from head to toe. Mouth grim. Silent.

Her arms wrapped tightly around herself as she tried to hold back her shivers. From the cold or fear? "You have a Jeremiah Johnson thing going on here? That was my dad's favorite movie." She nearly tripped over her tongue when his brilliant eyes flashed dangerously. "I'm trying to find Old Nick's Cabin. Can…can…can you help me?" *Damn teeth! Stop chattering!*

The stranger motioned toward the back porch. "You'd better go inside before you turn into a block of ice. The snow is coming down too hard to get there right now." He hung back, waiting for her to go first. Only when she hesitated at the door did he open it for her. "After you."

The heat wrapped around her like a warm blanket the instant she stepped inside. A soft sigh slipped out as she moved to the woodstove and held her hands over it, steam rising off her gloves and her coat. "Mmm. Thank you. This feels so good."

Her host silently put a cast iron kettle on the woodstove and handed her thick, warm socks. "You need to take off your wet coat and boots." He took them, shaking his head with a look of long-suffering, most likely due to their inadequacy, and handed her a blanket to wrap up in. He pulled off his boots and fixed two cups of piping hot coffee. He cleared his throat and held up the cream and sugar.

"Yes, please. Two sugars. Lots of cream." She could swear his lips quirked up at the corner for a fleeting second as he doctored her cup and left his black. He handed her a mug which felt like heaven to her nearly frozen fingers. He drew up a chair from the small table by the window to the woodstove and opened the door. He sipped at his cup and stared into the flames as motionless as a statue.

It prompted her to start babbling, trying to fill in the awkward lull. "I'm Stella. My father loved old movies. My name came from one of the best, *A Streetcar Named Desire*. He died when I was four, and my mom raised me alone from then on." She clammed up, wondering why she was laying bare her family history to a complete stranger.

"You could say my mother raised me alone, too." His lip curled down at the corners, a line forming between his eyes. Something burned deep in his gaze for an instant. He breathed out hard and looked into her eyes. "My name is Jesse."

He didn't give her anything else. She had a feeling it would be like pulling teeth to try to force anything out of him. His name and opening up his home would have to do. She shifted in her chair and sighed. Leaned back and raised her feet closer to the flames. She held back a groan. The heat felt *so* good. She closed her eyes and let it soak in as deep as it would go. Odd. She should have been on edge, alone, in a cabin in the woods, far from civilization with a man she'd never met before. Perhaps hypothermia and exhaustion had replaced her better judgement, but she felt safe and protected—

—like he would hold back the wolf at the door.

The chair beside her creaked. A gentle touch on her feet had her eyes snapping open. Jesse knelt beside her and cradled her right foot in his extremely large, unbelievably tender hands. He glanced up at her and for a moment, the shutters dropped, showing someone who looked very young and lost in a torment of his own. His voice was so low, she had to lean closer to hear him. "You need to get your circulation flowing, get the heat all the way down to your toes. You're lucky you didn't get frostbite. Those boots aren't meant for hiking in the snow." He tipped his head to the side, his eyes sliding sideways to the hook on the wall. "Neither is that coat." He moved from one foot to the other and sat back on his heels. "Do they feel all right?"

"Yes. Thank you." She sipped at her coffee, her gaze following him as he moved quietly around the small space, hardly making a sound. Setting the kitchen to rights. Filling the sink with hot water from the kettle sitting on the woodstove, adding soap. Letting it get sudsy. Picking up a rag to scrub fast and furious even though the water had to be hot enough to nearly peel the skin from his fingers.

When the last dish was in the drying rack on the counter, he peered out the window over the sink and let out a huff. He turned to face her, propping his hip against the sink. "Listen, there's no sign of this snow stopping, and now it's getting dark. I think you should wait it out here. I don't know if you realize it, but there's only a generator at your place, and I don't know if it's been fired up ahead of time for you. It's going to take time to shovel our way in, build a fire, warm the place up. You're welcome to my bed. I'll sleep on the floor or in the chair."

She stood up and joined him at the sink. She squinted but couldn't see anything but a wall of white. The thick shadow of darkness pressed in closer while flakes flew in front of the small battery-operated light on the porch. She couldn't imagine going out there *now*. When it came to choosing between snow falling at an alarming rate in the frigid air or the man beside her, she'd take her chances with a warm, dry cabin and a stranger. She peeked up at him from the corner of her eye. "I'll stay." It would give her one heck of a story. Besides, it gave her one hell of a view inside. Maybe he'd take his shirt off again—

—and something else for an encore.

Chapter Three

Jesse did his best to be civil. He cooked a can of stew on the woodstove, rationing propane for the cookstove—one less thing to pick up in town. He slathered butter on the crusty bread he bought at the store earlier that day. He stared out the window into the darkness, centering himself, and turned around, startled to find the table all set. "You didn't have to do that."

Stella shrugged. "My mama taught me to help out in any way I could when I was company."

Company. Something he never had. Too risky growing up in a house where they never knew what to expect. But he remembered, buried far beneath the bad memories, the times when he was little. His mother gave him tea parties. A precious slip of his life when she was able to share her unconditional love with nothing stopping her. Teaching him how to snuggle, chit chat, laugh, and have good manners.

Time to find them now.

He pulled out a chair and made a little bow. "Please sit." He turned on his battered radio, surprised to pick up a station with some old-time jazz. Thankful he could fill the silence. The stew bubbled quickly.

Relieved, he dished out two bowls, set them beside the bread, and poured two tall glasses of water.

"Cheers," Stella smiled shyly and raised her glass, clinking it with his before focusing on her steaming food.

Watching her lips purse as she blew on the stew did something to his insides. A sudden rush of heat went straight to his head. Light-headed, he almost spilled his glass. "Whoa." He caught himself and set his cup on the table. "Sorry. Don't know why I'm so clumsy tonight."

"You're not Superman, even if you are the closest to him I've ever met in person. You shouldn't work so hard out there. I'm going to let you in on a secret. That wood will still be there tomorrow. And the next day. And the next." Stella's hand fit his perfectly as she closed the gap between them. Pushing back the cold and darkness that had been chasing him since he climbed the mountain. *Who are you kidding?*

It's been chasing you for your entire life.

His voice was rough. "I like to stay busy." *You need to stay busy, or you'll go out of your mind.* "It keeps me from thinking about things I'd rather forget." Even though he'd never forget.

He scraped his bowl clean and put his dishes in the sink, adding the empty stew pot before putting the kettle on the woodstove. Again. Unwilling to stand around waiting for it and struggling to find anything to say to his visitor, *he went outside and carried in an armload of wood he didn't need.* Filled the woodstove. Started scrubbing the dishes hard enough to take the paint off them.

A light touch on his shoulder sent water splashing everywhere as the rag flew across the room. Stella pressed her palm to her chest, eyes wide. "I'm so sorry. I didn't mean to startle you."

He laughed self-consciously. "That's all right. I'm just not used to being around other people." He set the last dish in the drying rack and folded the towel neatly before turning toward her. He thrusted his hands in his pockets to keep himself from reaching out to find out if she was as soft as she looked or stepping in closer to find out if the amazing scent that made him dizzy came from her clothes, her skin, or her hair. *Or all three.* Mentally, he shook himself and gestured to the bathroom. "You're welcome to the bathroom first to get ready for bed. I'll be right out here if you need anything."

"Thank you." She grabbed the handle of her suitcase and rolled it in, closing the door behind her.

Restless and having no clue what to do with himself, he pulled out a thick comforter, grabbed a few extra blankets, and a pillow to spread out on the floor in the living room, on the braided rug, right by the woodstove. The sounds of movement coming from the bathroom couldn't let him think about anything else, wouldn't allow him to keep still. He paced and stopped at the window facing the mountains around him. He braced his hands against the sill and stared out into the darkness, the snow falling in a sheet. He beat down panic that it might never stop, trapping him with the woman only a few feet away.

No matter how beautiful she might be, she scared the hell out of him.

He hadn't had a good role model on how to treat a woman and hoped the basic instinct existed. Jesse thought it did with how hard he tried to take care of his mother. Still, he didn't trust himself to have a relationship of his own. Not now. Not anytime soon. Not ever. He'd been a loner growing up. Didn't plan on changing his personal make-up anytime soon. His fingers tightened on the windowsill until the wood started to creak. He closed his eyes and prayed. *Please. Give me strength.*

The bathroom opened and shut behind him, pulling him around to face Stella. She smiled. Her cheeks flushed as she did a curtsy in her modest flannel pajamas. "I'm glad I packed the right kind of sleepwear at least. It's too cold for anything else!"

Jesse couldn't hold back a chuckle. "The golden retrievers are a nice touch. They're my favorite." Something else he always wanted but his mother couldn't risk. His father couldn't be trusted with people. There was no way a dog could be allowed in their house. Forget bringing in *any* other living creature. Not even a goldfish. Jesse never even asked. He pushed those thoughts away, the tide of memories threatening to come flooding in, and took down the lamp hanging by the bathroom door. "This is battery operated. Keep it right by the bed in case you need it in the middle of the night. I'll be right here. I sleep light. Don't be afraid to wake me if you need anything. Have a good night, Stella."

"Good night. Thank you again. For everything." She turned away from the woodstove and slipped into bed, pulling the covers up until only her hair peeked out.

The sight of her tucked in snug made his body go lose. He took her lead, turned out the lights, and stretched out on the floor. He pinned his gaze on the flickering flames of the woodstove. He'd left the door open to provide a soft light. He thought it might help comfort her in a strange place with someone unfamiliar. *A stranger in a strange land.* He listened carefully. Her even breathing told him the story of how well she slept. And how still she was. The hike in must have exhausted her.

Sharing his small space wore him down to the bone, threatening to let her walk in and tear down the walls he'd carefully built in the last few months—

—make that all his life.

Jesse barely slept. Staring at dancing flames in the woodstove. Mulling over the presence of a stranger in his house and the fire she set deep in his core, creating an inferno hot enough to burn him to ash. He finally drifted off toward daybreak, lost in a raging blizzard in his dreams, jerked awake by a loud clanging in the kitchen. He scraped his hands over his face, but remained on the floor, silently following Stella's movements, peeking through narrow slits. She moved with grace, almost like she was in a dance, placing the percolator coffee pot on the woodstove, setting the table while it heated up, whipping out a cast iron frying pan to add butter, crack some eggs, add a dash of salt and pepper, and a few strips of bacon the way his mom would. Fixing him his first meal of the day like Mom used to do. Except the girl in his cabin moved with confidence, standing tall, wearing a smile. Not cringing, curled up, trying to be smaller.

Waiting for the blow to come out of nowhere.

She lit up when he threw back his covers and slowly stood up. "Good morning. I thought you'd be hungry."

"Thank you." He raked his fingers through his hair and stretched until his bones cracked. "I'll be right out." He stepped into the bathroom. Closed the door. Pressed his back against it and tried to remember how to breathe. Because her cheeks were rosy, her hair mussed, her smile reaching out to him like no one had in far too long. And he didn't know how to handle it. He pushed off, did his business, and washed up, brushing his teeth. Stared at his reflection, hands braced on the sink, shook his head. *What the hell are you doing?*

He stepped out and sat in the chair across from his houseguest. He picked up his fork and took a bite. His eyes widened, a grin finding its way to the surface. "This is really good. Your cooking talents outshine mine."

She blushed, the rush of color to her cheeks complementing the sparkle in her eyes. "Thank you. Breakfast is my specialty. My favorite meal of the day." She met his gaze only to duck her head and study her plate intently. The girl may have just woken up, hair pulled up in a loose knot on the top of her head, yet she looked remarkably put together *and* chipper. A steady stream of chatter filled the room. About the weather. The beauty of the view. The hike. The wildlife.

After six months in prison with little conversation except for mandated sessions with his assigned therapist, the flood of words set Jesse's head spinning. He nodded, mentally scrambling to keep up with each thread. He made brief comments here and there but didn't have it in him to say more. Not yet. Her words trailed off and she intensely studied her eggs, prompting him to offer her some sort of an explanation. "I'm sorry. I haven't been around people much for a good while. I really do appreciate you going to all this effort for me."

She flipped her hands in the air with a little laugh. "That's all right. I've always been someone who can't slow her tongue down. I don't expect everyone else to be the same way." Flustered, she stood and picked up the plates.

He shot up and took them from her hands. "Please. Let me take care of this. Go ahead and help yourself to anything you need in the bathroom." *Damn! Why do you have to sound so abrupt?*

She stepped back, lip quivering. "Thank you for opening your home to me. I know I was not part of your plans." She tilted her head to the side, forehead creased. "I'm sorry to invade your privacy. I'll get out of your hair as quickly as I can."

He set everything down and caught her hand, giving it a gentle squeeze. "Take your time. You're no problem being here. *Really.*" She nodded and left him to clean up, rummaging in her suitcase. A few minutes later, the water started running, the pitter patter on the shower floor filling his head with vivid images of the woman in the next room—without any clothes—images he had to push out of his mind. He washed dishes with gusto, partially to blot out the sound, partially to distract himself. Because he couldn't deal with the complications of a woman in his life right now.

He was having a hard enough time getting his crap together.

He set the last dish in the drying rack, folded the towel neatly on the edge of the sink. Exactly the way his mother folded it. Everything just so because that was how his father demanded it. He cursed under his breath and crumpled the towel up in a ball. "I'm ready. I guess we should get going." The quiet voice in his ear made him jump. Stella stepped back, hands up. "Sorry. I didn't mean to startle you."

How many times had he seen a woman with her hands raised as a protective shield?

A completely useless shield.

He shrugged, trying to cover his discomfort. Like it was completely normal to jump out of his skin simply because someone was in the same room with him. "I haven't been outside yet. Let's take a look and see what's going on out there." He opened the door and let out a long whistle. "We're not going anywhere." The snow had stopped, only a few flakes drifting in the air, carried by a gentle breeze. The storm might be over, but its aftermath hit hard. A blanket of white had completely hidden the steps, mounting until it piled up all the way to his porch.

"But I need to get to my cabin!" Stella knocked shoulders with him as she took in the view. "The storm is over. There must be *something* we can do."

Jesse gestured to his yard. "There is at least three feet out there! Going out now would be like trying to walk through a wall, and it's a perfect recipe for frostbite." As if on cue, the wind picked up with a mournful howl and a bite sharp enough to cut to the bone, pushing them inside. He shut the door and pressed his back against it. "I think we should wait it out a few hours. I'll tackle the snow here, see if the wind dies down. If it doesn't get better, you might have to stay another day." His spirits lifted at the prospect of some company. Maybe he *could* learn how to be around human beings again.

She whipped around to face him, jaw set like a bulldog, eyes flashing dangerously. The girl might be tougher than she looked. "You can't make me!"

"I am *not* hanging around here waiting for another day. If you won't help me, I'll make it by myself!" Stella suddenly had an overwhelming urge to get out. Get out *now*. She'd set herself on this path to find her way back to her writing, to pull herself together. To learn how to live without her mother. If she didn't leave now, she'd fail on all three counts.

But even more powerful was the need to get away from the man who may have opened his home but everything about him said, *Keep Out.* She angrily pulled on her boots and her coat, zipping it up to her chin. She pulled up her hood and slipped on her gloves, silently berating herself. *Wool gloves with pretty buttons on them! Seriously? The moment your hands get wet you'll be a candidate for losing some fingers. You are utterly unprepared to rough it. You should be smarter than this! Learn something from all the books you've written. Your characters would do better than you.*

As a top-notch author, she prided herself on doing all her own research for her novels. How she didn't manage to read up before heading out into the wilderness on her own was beyond her. Pitiful. Furious with herself, she stomped to the door with her suitcase, wobbling on her inadequate, high-heeled boots, and glanced over her shoulder. "Thank you again. I can find my own way from here. Don't trouble yourself with following me."

She stepped outside with her bag in hand. A strong gust of cold air blasted down her coat and threw back her hood. Her whole body shivered, teeth chattering. She'd be damned if she'd retreat down the mountain with her tail between her legs. Or be forced to go back inside. Time to prove she could take on this challenge by herself. Stella forged her way down the steps and sank into the snow almost to her hips. She could barely breathe as the frigid gusts sucked the air from her lungs. Panic threatened to set in as she shook hard enough to cause a personal avalanche.

Heaven, help me.

"Oh, hell." Jesse grabbed his heavy coat off the hook by the door and shrugged into it, stuck his knit hat on his head, and put another in his pocket because the fool of a girl didn't have one. He plunged his feet into his boots and pulled on a pair of gloves. He grabbed his spare parka off the hook because her pretty coat was paper-thin. He rushed out onto the porch and resisted the urge to laugh when he saw her stuck only a few feet away. Unable to move. A big attitude and streak of independence didn't take her far.

The blue tinge around her lips killed his sense of humor.

He took two giant steps toward her, only to rock back on his heels when she flung herself against him, her hands clinging to his chest. Sobbing. "Please help me! I'm f-f-*freezing!*"

"You aren't yet but it won't take long. The forecast on the radio just said it's supposed to drop to zero, and you are *definitely not* dressed for that." He pulled his spare coat around her shoulders, the hat over her head, and scooped her up in his arms. He swung around toward the porch. She burrowed in close. Smelling good. Feeling good.

Kicking up the slow burn in his gut.

He beat it down and carried her inside, setting her by the woodstove. *Again.* He built up the fire and left the door open. It really didn't make a difference in how much heat it produced but it was a mental thing. Seeing those flames gave him a sense of security, let the warmth seep into all the cold places deep inside. *This isn't about you. You can work out your problems some other time!* He grabbed her a blanket and took off her boots, soaked all the way through. He peeled off her socks and gave her a heavy pair of wool ones, pulling them on for her because her hands were trembling too much. "Th…th…thank you. I'm sorry I'm so much trouble. I'm an idiot!"

"You're not." He grabbed the coffee pot, set it on the back of the stove to stay warm, and poured her a cup of the hot brew, going heavy on the cream and the sugar. He thrust it in her hands, wrapping her fingers around it. "Sip that slow or you'll burn your tongue. Drink all of it. You *really* need to warm up. Are you trying to get hypothermia? In case you haven't noticed, there's no medical care around here. No cell phone. That's why it is best to stay put right now." He pulled off his coat and hung it up, put his hat on the hooks. Ran his hand through his long strands, pushing them out of the way with a sigh. He set his boots by the door and grabbed his own cup of coffee. "Get thawed out. I'll take care of the shoveling here. We'll have some lunch and then we'll work our way to your cabin. It's going to take a few hours."

"Thank you." She didn't say anything more but only seemed to shrink in on herself. He gritted his teeth. The last thing he wanted was to see another woman trying to make herself small. She accepted a bowl of soup and a sandwich, set her dishes in the sink when she was done, and wrapped the blanket around herself tightly. Her gaze fixed on the flames of the woodstove, expression brooding.

Jesse put on all his winter gear, prepared to face the elements. When he came in from shoveling, she was sound asleep. He stood at the kitchen sink, hip propped against it and studied her. The way her long, wavy light brown strands drifted past her shoulders. If her eyes were open, it would be like looking at honey gleaming in a jar as the sunlight danced off it. Her smile, when she smiled, was equally sweet. Like his mother's. Something he'd rarely seen in his life. He couldn't resist helping her.

No matter how much it hurt.

Stella suddenly sat up and stretched, taking in her surroundings. Glancing his way, her whole body seemed to deflate. She met his gaze without a hint of a smile. "I really am smarter than this. Honestly. Recent troubles have sent all my common sense out the window."

Jesse grabbed a chair from the kitchen table and sat down across from her, resting his elbows on his knees while he let the heat from the fire seep into his bones. He kept his voice quiet. "I know how life can throw you for a loop. Trust me. It's happened to me, too." He leaned forward and took her hand in his. "I've finished shoveling and the wind has died down. If we use snowshoes, I think we can make our way there now. If you want to wait it out, we can. You're welcome to stay as long as you need to. I know you don't know me, but I can promise you one thing. You *will* be safe with me. I can't stand to see a woman who is hurting."

She wiped away a tear trickling down her face and shook her head. "No one should ever hurt *anyone*, don't you agree?" He swallowed hard, fighting the urge to pull away, wondering how her opinion of him might change if she knew the truth about him. She cleared her throat nervously. "I would really like to try going today if that's all right with you."

"Okay. Whatever you want. Just hold on a moment before you get ready." He pulled a pair of boots out of the closet. "These will be big on you, but they'll do for now." He handed her the parka that had been waiting for him when he arrived only to save the day when his guest thrust herself into a wall of snow. "Take this too. You can borrow both for as long as you need. It doesn't matter if they are too big. The most important thing is that you're warm enough. I've experienced what it's like to be unprepared for the wintery conditions up here." When he couldn't sleep, he'd gone out into the cold with nothing but a t-shirt and pajama pants and his sock feet. Trying to freeze out the pain.

Nothing worked.

She sniffled and her lips quivered. "When I planned this trip, I figured it was early in the season, and I'd stay inside if the weather turned. I had no idea it would be like this." She gazed out the window at the path he'd shoveled heading into the wilderness. "How are we going to trudge through all that snow all the way to my cabin? The sign said it was two miles away." The pitch of her voice headed toward a wail.

He squeezed her hand. "Easy now. We're halfway there. Only a mile to go from here. I've got two sets of snowshoes to help us on our way. You can borrow one for as long as you're here. We'll bring a thermos of coffee, take our time, and make it through. Just let me get things straightened out around here, and we'll set off. Promise."

"Thank you. I'm sorry I overreacted." She leaned in and kissed his cheek.

It burned, like a brand.

He started and pressed his palm to his flaming skin, but the heat went far below the surface, diving deep into his heart. "Sorry. A kind touch has been scarce in my life. I'm not sure what to do with it." He bit his tongue. *Why did you tell her that?*

They set off right after lunch, a folding shovel on his back because he knew they'd be digging their way in when they made it to the cabin. The snowshoes were a godsend, allowing them to walk mainly on top of the snow, only sinking in a few inches. Still, their progress was slow.

A hike that would normally take about twenty minutes took over an hour. Halfway there, her snowshoes got tangled and she dropped to her knees. He grabbed her quickly and pulled her to her feet before her pants were soaked through, holding her until she was steady. She nodded. "I'm all right. Let's keep going." They trudged on, an Arctic blast of air chasing them relentlessly the entire way. Jesse gritted his teeth. His woodstove was calling him.

As if on cue, a curtain of snow dropped on them like someone had flipped a switch. He picked up the pace, cursing how clumsy snowshoes could be even though he could only praise them a moment before. He deliberated, pondering if Stella should remove hers. He could carry her on his back if he had to, leave her luggage behind, and go back for it later. Otherwise, they might get stranded, caught between the safety of his cabin and hers. "Do you want to take a break?"

She shook her head, jaw set, and pushed on, breath coming in hard pants the farther they went. He almost hit his knees with a prayer of thanks when the shadowy outline of the cabin loomed in the distance. His relief was short-lived. No smoke billowed from the chimney in welcome. No one had rolled out the red carpet for her arrival. For all he knew, the owner may have thought she'd cancel with the change in weather. Or the owner could be on the other side of the country in someplace warm and sunny with no clue that Old Man Winter had decided to show up early in the Adirondacks. There was nothing for it but to take care of it when they managed to get inside. *One step at a time.* "We made it."

Stella broke her focus on the ground in front of her to glance up. "Oh, thank God." She closed her eyes and leaned against a tree. "I was beginning to think we would never get here."

"Wait here, and I'll clear a path so you can get inside." He grabbed the shovel off his back and started throwing snow left and right, thankful it was a powdery fluff. By the time he reached the front door, beads of sweat dampened his hairline and ran down his back. He swept his sleeve across his forehead and turned to wave her inside.

She tromped forward on her borrowed snowshoes, a bit awkward, but clasping her hands together in excitement as soon as she reached the porch. Anticipation stained her cheeks an even deeper shade of crimson than the cold air ever could. Her smile flashed, brighter than the sun. "It's perfect!" The porch was decorated with pine garland, snowshoes with a large plaid bow in red, green, and gold hanging over the door. The twinkling lights of a pine tree standing inside by the window cast a soft, white glow. Matching white lights were strung on the porch and a few of the surrounding trees. Stella's eyes were as wide as a child's as she took it all in. "*This* is the place. Life has snuffed out my Christmas spirit. I'm hoping here, I can light the flame again." Her eyes were wet, glistening, her tears on the brink of falling.

Her pain pulled at him, drawing him closer. He set his hand on hers, longing to help her. All his life, he'd wanted nothing more than to help the woman who mattered most to him. Maybe this time he could actually do something. Make a difference. "What happened?"

The glow in her eyes dimmed, her face tight. "I lost my mom."

He nodded, eyes burning. "So did I." It suddenly hit him. He would probably never see his mother again. A price he was only too willing to pay to keep her safe. He clamped down on his emotions and squeezed her hand. "What do you say we go inside? Let me get a fire going to warm you up."

She held on tight, ducking under his arm and letting him guide her inside. Their breath floated in a cloud around them. Jesse shivered as they stepped into the cabin. Somehow it was colder inside than outside. He turned, braced both hands on the door and managed to fight it closed. He leaned against it, catching his breath. Wondering how he could make it through this season if he'd have to fight his way through the weather day in and day out. He turned and pulled off his gloves, rubbed his hands together. He found a box of matches on the mantel, lit the oil lamp, built up the fireplace, threw in the tinder, and lit another match. He let the air hiss beneath his teeth when the flames reached up high, licking the stones of the fireplace, sending out sought- after heat. He stood by it. Sighed. Wanted to crawl inside. Jesse still wasn't accustomed to the cold. The steam started to rise off his coat.

Stella explored her temporary home. He studied her when a book on the table by the window caught his eye. "New York Times best seller" was splashed across the cover in sprawling letters, a name at the bottom, Stella Blair. A note sat propped next to it. *I hope you enjoy your stay. Would you please sign?* He flipped it over. The picture matched the starry-eyed girl who showed up at his doorstep. He glanced up at her standing beside him, cheeks burning. "That's me. Don't tell anyone you've found me. It's a secret."

"Don't worry. I came here to get away from people. There's no one to tell up here, and if anyone heads our way, I'm the first stop. I'll send them packing." He stoked the fire. Checked the wood pile by the door on the porch. Made sure all the oil lamps and battery-operated lamps worked. Last, he checked the fridge and cabinets. He nodded in satisfaction. They were all fully stocked. "There. I think you're set. You have enough food to hold you over for some time, and if you need something you can always check in with me. I go into town every two weeks. Happy to get you something if you need it." Sweat beaded up on his forehead as the heat of the fireplace hit him. He wiped it away. "It's pretty toasty in here now. I'll leave you to get settled in."

She leaned in and hugged him. "Thank you so much for getting me here—and for being so patient with me." She reached in her pocket. "Let me pay you."

He waved her off. "That isn't necessary. If you need anything, you know where to find me."

She grabbed his sleeve. "Wait. I can't send you out without at least returning some of your hospitality. Let me get you a cup of tea." She put the kettle on the propane stove and set out two cups. She gestured to a cozy table by the window. "Have a seat." She rooted around and clapped her hands. "Sweet. The girl even made me some cinnamon bread." She sliced two generous pieces and set them on a plate. As soon as the kettle whistled, Stella filled the cups and set them on the table with a little pitcher of cream and a sugar bowl. "There. Isn't this just like home sweet home?"

He crossed his arms over his chest as his eyes scanned the interior, his jaw set. "You're really cut off from everyone here. No phone. Looks like they've got you set up with propane to generate your electricity and heat. If you run out of propane or have any problem with your system, you could be in trouble. I'm going to check in on you to make sure you're all right."

"Why don't we make it Sunday mornings? I'll make breakfast." Her smile lit a flame inside of him. They ate in companionable silence, and all the while, he couldn't help but think how much better life could be with someone like her in it. The kind of life he'd always wanted, dreamed about, but never thought he could have.

As soon as he finished, Jesse gathered the plates. "Habit," he told her with a sideways grin as he put them in the sink, catching a dish that almost dropped on the floor. Tremors ran through his hands. He gripped the edge and breathed hard through his nose.

Growing up, he learned fast to pick up or he'd get a whack up the side of his head.

"It's snowing again. Are you sure you don't want to wait it out here? The sofa pulls out into a bed." Stella stood with her arms wrapped around her waist by the French doors overlooking the back deck. She glanced over her shoulder. "You've got to be exhausted. I don't like to think about you freezing out there or getting stuck in a drift after all you've done for me."

Jesse pushed off from the sink and plastered on a smile. "Thanks, but there's no need, really. The snow's light. I'll be all right." He pulled on his boots and his coat quickly. He had to leave and leave now. Warmth, comfort and companionship would be hard to resist. It was the type of life he always wanted but could never have. And maybe he didn't deserve it.

She walked him to the door, her hand waving like a flag as he trekked back through the snow. Her voice drifted after him. "Thank you again for helping a damsel in distress. You're the stuff that novels are made of." If only she knew the whole truth. She wouldn't write him as the hero.

He'd be the villain.

Chapter Four

Jesse had to fight himself every day to keep himself from going to Stella's cabin to check in on her. Chomping at the bit, at war with his inner attraction to her and the need to leave her alone. She was here to work, not to get distracted by him. He filled his days with as much walking, climbing, chopping, stacking, and scrubbing as he could, trying to wear himself out. Nights were the hardest. Before bed, the pacing set in because he was so on edge. He had to wear his body down to slip into a deep sleep. Failing, he stared at the ceiling long into the night, eyes burning. Sometimes until the sky lightened outside his window and he might as well get up. His mind filled with awful pictures of what might have befallen her in the days in between. His past made it all too easy to send his imagination on a path to terrible places. His longing for her was twisted up with his fear. He couldn't forget her smile. Or the shine in her eyes. Or the way her hair grazed her shoulders, her cheek. The feel of her soft touch on his hand made him want to be close to her. Somehow, he waited it out until Sunday—the longest week of his life.

Jail had nothing compared to the power of a woman.

"You made it. Right on time!" Stella stood on the porch, hair falling in soft waves around her face. She was swallowed up by a snowy white sweater a few sizes too big. Dark leggings revealed the curves in her legs. Thick socks came up to her knees with fluff around the top. Her breath drifted out in a cloud, roses blooming in her cheeks, her bright eyes snapping with vitality. Cabin life looked good on her.

One of the prettiest things he'd ever seen.

She set him off kilter. He grabbed the railing to steady himself before mounting the steps. Fighting to find his center. "I told you I'd be here. I keep my promises." After a lifetime of being the victim of broken promises, it was a vow he'd made to himself to *never* let anyone down because *he* didn't keep his word. He reached the top step and held out a package. Heat crept up his neck to his cheeks as she opened it, oohing and ahhing appropriately. "Homemade chocolate chip. I've tried my hand at baking this week. The birds enjoyed a feast or two, but this batch was passable." He rubbed his belly. "I tested them myself."

She picked one and took a big bite, her smile blooming. "They're delicious! We'll have some of these for dessert. Come on in. I hope you brought your appetite."

He stepped inside and pulled off his boots. She took his coat, immediately filling him with a warm sense of welcome. He couldn't help smiling. The table was loaded with food: pancakes, bacon *and* sausage, scrambled eggs, home fries, toast, and jam. "Wow! You went all out!"

It was the kind of breakfast his mother made for Christmas morning—or any time to celebrate when his father was away for any length of time. And he always secretly hoped his old man would get lost, sidetracked, distracted by another girl, another home, another life and never come back.

She pulled out a chair for him, filled his coffee cup, and finished preparing her own cup. She pushed the fixings his way after making her coffee light and sweet, just like the girl. "I like to cook breakfast, any time of the day. Some of my best memories are from when my mom would make breakfast for dinner. When Dad was away or working late, I could count on eggs, bacon, French toast or a tower of pancakes. It was our special treat, something between her and me. We'd sit in the living room to eat, something we never did. Dad believed in eating at the table. We wore our pajamas. We put out blankets and pillows on the rug. We would watch some of our favorite movies. If I was really lucky, we'd have a slumber party." Her eyes suddenly filled as she sniffled. "When Daddy died, Mom made a breakfast dinner and tucked me in next to her on the couch all night. She never let go."

He wondered what that might be like, to have a household of light that wasn't weighed down by the dark shadow of fear even though it had been dimmed by grief.

"It sounds like you had an amazing mother." He filled his mouth with some of Stella's delicious food because he didn't have anything to say. Good memories in his childhood—and life, for that matter—were few and far between. When he'd polished off his plate, he gave her a smile in return. "Everything was really good, just like Mom liked to make." Because she did. She wanted to give him the world. His eyes burned, thinking of those moments, snug against her side while she rocked him back and forth, whispering loving words to make up for the chaos whenever she could. He glanced out the window to avoid meeting Stella's gaze. His eyes went wide. "Wow. You really have done a lot of shoveling." He glanced at her. "You look like such a little thing. I wouldn't think you had it in you."

"Well, you can't judge a book by its cover." She stood up and braced her hands on the windowsill. "You should see out back to the woodpile and beyond. I made it a good way up the trail. I'll keep plugging away at it, see how far I can go before the next snowstorm has me back at square one." She sighed heavily, a line forming between her eyes. "I have a lot of time on my hands here. I can only write for so many hours. *If* I can think of something to write. Shoveling gives me something to do." Her habitual grin reappeared as she flexed her biceps. "It builds muscles, too."

Jesse shook his head. It was hard to keep this one down. The moment she reached for the plates, he shot up and cleared them for her. "I told you. Mom always said I should help out." *Because at least one man in her home would be a gentleman if he ever had the chance to get out, to go someplace else. Someplace better. How she prayed he would find something better one day.* "Looks like you've been brushing up on your cooking skills too." He tapped the platter of cookies and wrapped up a loaf of bread on the counter with a wink.

She joined him at the sink and stood hip to hip as he filled it with hot water. The luxury of propane to heat a water tank made household chores much easier. He waited for the bubbles to lather up and started scrubbing with gusto, mentally railing against the man who failed to raise him. Someone who wasn't remotely like a *gentle* man. His mouth twisted in aggravation. He had to wrestle it into a straight line. A smile wasn't going to happen, not with the bitter taste in his mouth and the knot in his stomach. Stella took each dish and dried it. "You *really* don't have to do this. You're my guest."

"My mother taught me to always lend a hand, *especially* when you are a guest." When the last dish was washed and put away, he wiped his hands on his pants. "Well, it looks like you're all set. I'll get out of your hair."

She grabbed his hand, pulling him toward the living room before he could leave. "Do you really have to hurry back?" She blushed. "It's just… I get a little lonely here. How about we listen to the radio? Talk a bit?"

The knot in his gut gave a sharp tug. Talking was one thing he didn't want to do. *Couldn't* do. He had nothing to talk about, at least not with her. Talking was one skill he'd never mastered in his life, not when it came to small talk, or the big stuff—or anything in between. Because it was just *too damn hard.* And then she turned those beautiful amber eyes his way and his reluctance melted away. He only wanted to give her something. *Anything.* He cleared his throat. "I can stay for a little while, but not too long. You never know when the weather will turn." That wasn't a lie. The clouds gathering on the horizon didn't look promising.

Stella patted the loveseat by the window. He sank down beside her, easing his way into the cushion. Close enough for her thigh to press against his. Sending him off kilter, his pulse skittering. He glanced at her face and noticed a light dusting of freckles, like someone had dipped a brush in a golden powder and dabbed it on her cheekbones. Her breath kissed his skin as she leaned across him to turn the knob on the radio. Soft music drifted through the air, filling the room. Something old. Something from an all-Jazz station. The Glenn Miller Band.

She rested against the cushions and closed her eyes, a smile stretching from ear to ear. "Beautiful. My grandfather was right. This is music that transcends time." Before he could think of something to say in response, she darted to her feet and held out her hand. "Dance with me."

It wasn't a question. Besides, he couldn't tell her no. That would be too rude, dampening the glow in her eyes, snuffing out her smile. He'd spent a lifetime trying to keep the light flickering in his mother's eyes. An uphill battle and nearly a lost cause. Like trying to keep a candle burning outside in the middle of a hurricane. He couldn't hurt this girl. He didn't understand it. He hardly knew her.

But it felt like she'd been a part of him for a lifetime.

He took her outstretched fingers, closing his much larger hand around hers, and stood. Unsteady, heart fluttering, trying to remember how to breathe. The girl stole his sense of balance, rocked him to the core. He cleared his throat. "I'm not a very good dancer."

She smiled. "There's no such thing as a bad dancer. Just let your body move with the music, anywhere you want it to go. Or don't, stand still—it's completely up to you." She hummed the melody, stepped in close, and tucked her head under his collarbone. Her arms wrapped around his waist and held on tight. "Mmm. This is nice. Really nice. I can't remember the last time someone danced with me."

No one had ever danced with him. Yet, he swayed with her. Back and forth, back and forth, letting her humming vibrate in his chest and fill all the empty places. He set his chin on the top of her head and closed his eyes. Still moving even when the song came to an end. "I don't want to stop."

She lifted her head, and her fingers trailed along his jaw, up his cheek, through his hair. "Who said you have to? You can dance with me for as long as you want."

The next song began. They continued to move in a circle, their steps slowing, her head tipped up. Trapping him in her gaze. Slower and slower. Something shifted inside of him as his head tilted down and she met him halfway, her mouth connecting with his. His eyelids drooped shut, bursts of light exploding behind them, like fireworks. His hands tightened around her shoulders, a thrumming starting in his chest. Getting stronger. Stronger. Louder. Making him dizzy. His eyes opened. She gazed at him, scarlet streaks staining her cheeks. He broke free, gasping for breath, and stepped back. "I'm sorry. Sorry. I shouldn't have done that."

Her hand found its way to his. Held on tight. "You didn't. *I* did."

He moved away, spun around, fumbled to get his boots and coat on. "But I should've stopped it. Stopped you. I'm sorry. I've got to go."

She followed him to the open door, grabbed his arm and gave it a tug. "You didn't do anything wrong. I'll see you. In one week. If you don't come, I'll come to you."

His heart lurched in his chest. The thought of her stepping inside his cabin, now that he knew what power she had over him, was too much. He nodded with a jerk. "In one week. I'll be here."

He stepped out onto the porch and hurried down the path, back the way he came. Something—the good manners instilled in him by the only other woman who mattered to him, or the emotions threatening to drown him—pulled him around one last time to lift his hand in a wave. Stella waved back just as snow began to fall. So fast, so heavy, so thick, it created a curtain, blocking her from view. It was the only reason he could move. He took a gulp of air, able to breathe again, and turned around to hurry home.

Dousing his head with cold water the moment he stepped through the door.

Jesse shoved his feelings for his neighbor deep inside of him. Locked them up tight where they belonged, setting himself to one hard task after another. If he was exhausted, maybe he could sleep. Stop thinking about her. Every minute of the day. And all the seconds in between. As the weather grew colder and the snow mounted, the need for firewood grew. He chopped harder, longer, carted more wood, stacked it higher, walked farther every day. When he looked in the mirror, someone even leaner and more honed stared back at him.

Whittling him down like something carved out of wood or stone.

He gripped the sink as hard as he could. Panic welled up inside of him, tremors hitting him hard. He wanted to wipe away *every* trace of himself. He picked up his razor only to drop it. He bowed his head, eyes squeezed shut. His stomach clenched, *everything* tight. "Not going to get far shaking like that…except maybe to kill yourself." He raised his head and met his reflection's gaze. "*You can do this,*" he growled through gritted teeth. He lathered on a heavy layer of shaving cream and took the first swipe. And another. Scissors finished the transformation as he pulled out one strand of hair, then another, snipping away. Bits of hair fluttered through the air, coating the sink and the floor.

He took a step closer and leaned into the mirror with a nod of approval. A stranger stared back at him that had never been there before. *Out with the old, in with the new.* He was happy to leave who he used to be behind. He never wanted to see that man again—

—or the man who ruined him instead of raising him.

His eyes glittered dangerously thinking about his father. He rammed his hands against the sink, whipped around, and slammed his fist on the door. He stormed out of the bathroom, smothered by the tiny confines of his cabin. Most days it suited him. Snug. Comfortable. Giving him everything he needed. But on a day like today, it was a cage.

Jesse yanked on his outdoor gear. Anger, frustration, and worry churned inside of him, on the brink of an eruption, propelling him down the mountain. On a mission for supplies, he was out of sorts the moment he stepped inside the general store. The *only* place to shop for necessities in town. Restocking his cupboards wasn't his priority. A phone call meant more than food or water; it meant peace of mind.

To make sure his mother was okay.

He called at different times, depending on when he managed to get to town. A fight against the elements might slow him down but nothing could make him give up. He used a different name every time he called her. Mary. Jenny. Amelia. Nothing close to his mother's name. Jesse never said who was calling. He hung on to every ring, heart pounding, breath caught in his throat. The need to hear her voice strong enough to hurt, gnawing at his insides. Wondering what he'd do if she didn't answer. Every time she did, he sagged with relief.

Five minutes. That's all they had before he hung up. He was probably paranoid. He didn't care. Jesse didn't want to give anything away to her monster. *Their* monster. The man he grew up with sucked the life and joy out of their home. Jesse swore he would *never* be anything like his old man—

—only to be proven wrong the day his fists pummeled his father's face beyond recognition.

His hand shook hard as he clung to the phone. Damn the tremor in her voice. "Love you, baby," just about broke him every time.

He whispered, "Love you to the moon and back," before hanging up the receiver. He wiped the cuff of his flannel sleeve across his face. Picked up his backpack, filled to the brim, and hoisted it on his shoulder. *Feels heavier this time*. He'd picked out a few things for Stella. Judging by the state of her cupboards, she'd be going hungry. Couldn't have that. She was perfect in every way. Couldn't stand bony women. He'd grown up watching his mother whittle down, nearly disappearing before his eyes. He needed something to hold on to.

If he ever had a woman to call his own.

He stepped outside and shifted his pack, welcoming the weight. Anything to keep the wolves at the door of an overcrowded mind, filled with far more painful memories than any young man his age should have—or at any age.

He worked his way back up the mountain, grateful to take on the challenge, trudging through a fresh layer of snow, watching the cloud of his breath float away. Halfway there, the skies opened, dumping a freezing blanket of white on his head. Some went down his neck, sending a shiver rippling down his spine. He slipped and slid from time to time and wrenched his knee. He had to pause, bent over at the waist, hands braced on his thighs, waiting for the fiery pain to die down to dull embers.

You really need to concentrate, watch where you put your feet. You can't afford to be careless. A sprain or a break would strand him in the wilderness. No one would be coming for him. Reaching his place, he stood by his wood stove, hands on his hips. *Just breathe.* He was getting worn down, tired to the bone. *Trying to forget about…her.* Impossible.

Jesse took care of his supplies first, putting everything away before he headed out again although he'd have preferred to stay put to let the heat soak in instead of facing the cold again. Sometimes, it went straight through him, giving him a chill that took hours to go away. There was nothing for it. Stella needed to be prepared for anything. The pack on his back grew heavier with every step. He would have dropped at his neighbor's cabin if she didn't have a sturdy railing to hold him up. He took a deep breath, bracing himself for her appearance, and raised a hand that dropped with weariness. He dredged up the strength and will to pick it up again and gave a solid rap on the door.

Stella pulled it open so quickly, he fell inside, catching himself on a table against the wall. "What? Have you been hanging around just waiting for me?" She was impossibly cute with her hair pulled up in a loose knot on the top of her head, glasses perched on her nose, a pen tucked behind her ear. The perfect match for his mental image of what an author should be. A scarlet sweater, big enough for him, swallowed her up with snowflakes scattered all over it. Her black leggings showed off her curvy legs, tall wool socks stretching almost to her thighs. For a flash, the temptation of running his finger to that dip behind her knees was almost too strong to resist. He clung to the table with everything he had. *Lord, give me strength—*

—or take me now.

"Oh my!" Stella pressed her hand to her mouth even though mischief sparked in her eyes. "You look like a yeti! Come thaw out right now!" She grabbed his arm and dragged him toward the living room.

He dropped his pack, propping it against a door. His feet found the way to the fireplace all by themselves. He closed his eyes and savored the warmth of the dancing flames, choking down a groan that threatened to crawl up his throat. "Oh, that feels *so* good. I could climb in."

She peeled off his coat, hat, and gloves, hanging them on hooks close to the fireplace. Steam drifted up from the damp material as soon as the warmer air hit them "That might be just a little bit too toasty." She took his hand and led him to a chair close to the flames "Sit! Sit! You're like a block of ice! What are you doing here? It's not your regular day."

The cold hit him down deep, sending tremors from his head to his toes. His teeth chattered uncontrollably. "I…had to…get…my supplies. Thought you could use…some. Your cupboards looked like Old Mother Hubbard's. Good thing you don't have a dog. Poor thing would starve. Couldn't let you wither away out here…all by your lonesome." He laced his fingers together over his knee and tried to stop the shaking. The only thing that could help him was enough time to thaw out.

She kissed his cheek. "Thank you for thinking about me." Her gaze traveled over him. She nodded in approval. "The new look is nice. I like seeing your face. You were hidden before." One finger grazed the long strands of hair brushing his collar. "Just need a bit more of a trim." She stood up. "You must stay for dinner and after, I'll give your haircut the finishing touches. It used to be my calling." When he started to stand up, she gently pushed him back. "Oh no you don't. You rest. If you could take on the journey through this kind of weather," a loud rumble only reiterated her point, "I can make you dinner. It's not every day you experience thunder snow. One bowl of chicken noodle soup with crusty bread coming up. I made both this morning."

Minutes later—or was it hours?—she nudged his shoulder. He'd nodded off, his chin on his chest. A tray waited for him on his lap with something in a bowl that smelled like heaven. He took a spoonful, broke off a bit of bread, and dipped it. His eyes closed with sheer pleasure. "Mmm. So good."

"I made it with my own little hands." She stood by his side, whisking away the bowl when it almost dropped to the floor.

"Sorry. I'm so tired." His eyelids and head drooped, his *whole body* heavy. Jesse couldn't budge if he wanted to.

"Lean on me." Stella tucked herself under his shoulder and helped him to the love seat across from the fireplace. "Lay your troubles down for a while and rest your head. Everything will still be waiting for you when you wake up." She pulled a blanket up to his chin. Ran a hand through his hair…and his eyelids closed. A fleeting sense of fear told him he should get up, get out as fast as he could. But darkness and the sweet release of sleep came for him first.

Stella knelt beside the man in her cabin. The only man she could think of. The only one she wanted. He'd begun sneaking his way into her stories. Had her planning a brand new one that revolved around him. She watched his chest rise and fall steadily. Up and down. She lifted her hand, tempted to skim her fingers over his cheeks, red from the cold. Curious if they were smooth or rough with stubble. She thought about trailing them through his hair. Trembled. He looked handsome clean-shaven, undeniably so, and yet she loved the rugged unkempt stranger she'd met in the beginning. She couldn't resist. Her fingers gently flitted over his hair. Warmth ran through her as his mouth quirked up at the corners and he made a small sound of contentment. Like a cat curled up by the fire.

She wanted to curl up with him.

Instead, she sat on the floor at his side, snug in a quilt, making sure his chest continued to fall slow and steady as he sighed heavily His body went loose, letting his guard down—for now. She unraveled a bit at the sight of him, his proximity, the energy that pulsed off him like a forcefield. And yet she winced. It seemed like he'd built a wall around himself, keeping others out instead of letting them in. Never allowing anyone to get to the heart of him. She bit her lip at the sight of the dark shadows under his eyes. Her index finger barely grazed the lines etched deeply at the corner of his eyes and in the brackets around his mouth. Her heart ached. She didn't know what he was running from or pushing away, why he was wearing himself to the point of no return.

She covered him with a blanket and settled her back against the couch, by his chest. Reassured by the soft sound of his breathing as she gazed into the dancing flames. She'd have to do something to help him. She resisted the urge to curl up beside him and tucked her legs beneath her. She sipped her tea slowly, picked up her pen, and tried to wend her way through her novel.

But all roads led back to him.

Chapter Five

Stella groaned, her hand coming up to knead a major kink in her neck. The hard floor didn't help her butt either. She shifted and glanced at the fireplace. It had died down to crimson coals buried deep down under a few charred pieces of wood, coated with ashes that floated around the dancing sparks. Otherwise, the room was dark. The sun had gone down.

Soft snoring in her ear propelled her to her feet, her palm pressing against her chest and her fluttering heart. Jesse slept on, his exhaustion finally getting the best of him as his body gave in. She tapped her lip with her pen, pondering what to do about it. Wake him and send him out in the cold or leave him sleeping on her couch? She didn't like option number one. Stella had a feeling *he* wouldn't like option number two.

She tiptoed over to the window and glanced outside. The snow she could feel and taste in the air, see in the low, heavy clouds that couldn't hold on to their burden, came down in a sheet. A sheet so thick there was no getting past it. She shook her head. No way, no how would she send him out there. He was very capable. That didn't mean he was impervious to the trials and tribulations that came with the approaching winter season in the mountains.

She draped her quilt over him, tossed enough logs on the fire to hold them over until morning—nothing worse than flitting across a cold floor with bare feet in the middle of the night to build up the fire because it was freezing. She shivered at the thought. Giving the cabin a quick once over, she found her way to the bedroom and quicky changed into modest, flannel pajamas. Her hand lingered on her doorknob. She considered closing it, thought better of it. An open door would let the heat in, and her guest if he became lonely or disoriented, lost, or attracted to her...

She'd help him to find his way.

She pulled up the covers to her chin and turned toward the living room, mesmerized by the shadowy outlines of the flames as they danced on her walls, listening intently. The howling of the wind blocked out the sound of her visitor's breathing. She wanted to set out blankets on the floor at his side. To make sure he was okay—and still there. *Don't push your luck. If he wakes up now, in your living room, he'll make a beeline for the door. You'll find his frozen body halfway between your place and his.*

The air hissed between her teeth as she closed her eyes. She thought about all the people who mattered to her, her next novel, what she'd do in the morning, what she wanted to do to her guest.

Stella Grace Blair. Stop dipping your toe in the deep end before you drown.

She turned over with a huff, resolutely putting her back to the fire, the man in her home, fighting to rein in her imagination. Eventually, the fresh air, the shoveling, and the hour caught up with her.

She didn't open her eyes again until morning when the sun poked at her eyelids, telling her to get up. A moan from the next room shifted her into high gear, scrambling to wrap a blanket around herself as she plunged her feet into slippers. She popped into the next room and put on the brakes as a rather tall, quite formidable figure loomed over her fireplace. Hands on his hips, glowering, giving a sasquatch competition, he turned her way, his eyes flashing. "What the *hell* am I doing here?"

Jesse's body was heavy, but pleasantly so, weighed down by the first deep sleep he'd had in…he didn't remember how long. Coming to the surface as the morning tried to shake him awake was like swimming through quicksand. He didn't budge. Didn't open his eyes. Didn't do anything. Just listened to the crackle of the fireplace, savoring the heat seeping all the way to his bones—something else that rarely happened. Being outside so often meant never truly getting warm.

Something pricked at the back of his mind like an annoying splinter, robbing him of his sense of tranquility. Something wasn't right. He squeezed his eyes shut and forced them to open. Sucked in a deep breath, a fist closing around his lungs. This wasn't his place. Wasn't where he belonged, not here with a woman he barely knew. He came up in a rush and threaded his hands through his hair. He gave a sharp tug and glanced down at his clothes. His body sagged in relief.

At least he still wore clothes.

He glared at the fireplace as the blood rushed to his head. His heart pounded in his chest, the echo of every beat thundering in his ears. The padding of soft footsteps spun him on his heels. He set his jaw, his gaze boring into the woman who stepped into the room. "What the *hell* am I doing here?" She seemed to shrink in on herself, giving the knot in his stomach a guilty tug, but he ignored it. He was in the right. "I shouldn't be here. You should have woken me up and sent me home…or at least you could have given me the choice to stay or leave on *my* terms. Not yours." He crossed his arms and turned around to glower at the fireplace.

"I didn't want to disturb you." She cleared her throat nervously and took a step toward him. He had to admire her. Most women, including his mother, would have backed away from him. "I could see you were completely done in. You're pushing yourself too hard. You need to give yourself a break or it's going to break you."

He drew himself up to his full height, shoulders back, jaw set, staring her down. "That's my choice to make and mine alone." He stomped across the room and yanked on his boots with jerky movements, followed by his coat, hat, and gloves. He made it as far as the door when he stopped, head down, palm pressed against it, pushing the air out through his nose. He turned around to face his hostess and almost crossed the room to take her in his arms.

The girl looked deflated, her arms wrapped around her waist, her face pale, eyes glistening. He'd hurt her. *Damn*! He never meant to hurt her. He throttled his voice down low. It cracked as he forced the words out. "Listen, I appreciate your hospitality. I really do. It's just my freedom was taken away from me for far too long with someone else calling the shots for my every move. I can't let that happen again. I *won't*. Ever. So, if there's a situation like this in the future, wake me up. Let me make up my own mind. Even though I'm stubborn as hell and I'm likely to take two steps forward and three steps back." He grabbed the doorknob and pulled it open, a cold gust of wind skittering in, bringing a dusting of snow with it. "*Please*. That's all I ask." His face twisted and his voice shook.

He plunged into the bitter chill of early morning. The sun had just begun its climb up the sky. It couldn't be much later than six or so, not really such a violation. Jesse knew Stella meant well, that her heart was in the right place, but still couldn't stomach being there without his knowledge or permission. He didn't trust what could happen in such close quarters with a woman after being on his own for most of his life—

—especially with a woman like Stella.

He trudged through the deep snow without stopping the entire way home, trying to douse the flames of anger licking at his insides. He tried to put the image of her face, the pain he'd stamped on it, out of his mind. By the time he hit his doorstep, he was gasping for breath, his hand pressed to a fierce stab in his side that had him bent over when he walked through the door. He stood still with his hands braced on his knees, waiting it out, shivering. The woodstove had gone out. He cursed under his breath and stomped some more, opening the door of the stove, grabbing a pile of wood and hurling it inside. He threw in some tinder and wads of paper before striking a long match. It took several tries to get it to catch, standing there quaking, his clothes dripping, a puddle forming on the floor. His teeth chattered, and the heat of the anger in his core intensified, threatening to melt him down.

He peeled off his gloves with his teeth, tossed them on the floor, and held his hands in front of the flames. As the warmth seeped in, the tension flowed out of his muscles. His fury went with it. He shed his coat and hung it on the hook by the door, took off his boots and set them by the woodstove to dry off. His stomach grumbled. *Should have at least stayed for breakfast. She's a good cook.* The thought made him smirk.

He put the kettle on the woodstove and paced while he waited for it to whistle. He filled a cup with steaming water and a teabag. He took oatmeal out of the cabinet, made a double batch. He hooked a chair with his foot and pulled it right up to the fire. A fine tremor ran through him. He just couldn't get warm, even after the tea and the hot cereal. He set his dishes in the sink and grabbed a few blankets, wrapped them tightly around himself like a mummy and crawled into bed. The shaking continued, hard enough to rattle the bed and his bones. His head began to pound. Everything ached. Sweat trickled down his forehead, his hair sticking to his temples. He brushed the back of his hand over his cheek. Winced. *Great. Now you're burning up. Great way to be Mr. Independent.*

With luck like his, someone would find his bones in his bed some months from now and that would be the end of him.

A loud thumping on the door made Jesse jerk so hard he almost rolled off the bed. He lay there in the middle of the mattress, staring at the woodstove, the door open, thankfully the flames still burning. Because there was no way in hell he could drag himself out of bed, crawl to the door, and muscle some wood—even one piece—to the stove. He knew the room had to be warm. The little stove did its job well and made the snug little cabin a cozy place that could weather any storm. *Why am I as cold as ice?* His fists clenched as he tucked himself into a ball, desperately trying to get warm.

The thumping came again. "Jesse? Are you there? I'm worried about you."

He moaned. The sound of her voice, no matter how concerned, stabbed at his brain. "Go away. Please."

"That's it. I'm coming in." The door swung open so hard it hit the wall. He moaned again. Every sound was like a brick being thrown at his head. Stella, bundled up to her eyebrows, stepped inside, stomping some more.

"Will you please, *for the love of God*, stop making so much noise?" His voice was gravelly. *Wonderful.* Now his throat hurt like he'd swallowed sandpaper and a mouthful of glass.

Her eyebrows drew together while she peeled off her outer gear. "I had a feeling something was wrong. You're sick, aren't you?" She crossed the room and peered closely at him, pressing her hand to his forehead, pulling it back like she'd been singed. "You're *really* sick."

His hand shot out, nearly missed, his vision blurry. He caught her, drew her in close enough to bury his head in her waist. His arms wrapped around her. "Please. Don't leave. Don't leave me alone."

Jesse sat up fast, scrambling to hold on to the shreds of his dream but they scattered. He *was* on fire. His shirt was sopping and stuck to his skin. He peered through the darkness, drawn to the red embers burning in his woodstove, the door open, barely kicking out any heat. He cursed, threw the covers back and stumbled across the room. He threw a few logs in, emptying the rack against the wall. *Have to get more.* The thought drifted fuzzily through his brain, but he didn't want to step outside, not now. It was freezing—*below* freezing—outside, so cold his windows were frosted over. He wilted in relief when the wood caught immediately. The coals were hotter than he thought. *Like you.*

He filled a glass at the faucet and guzzled it down. Took down the ibuprofen, struggling to remove the cap in the dark. "Where's the damn notch?" He growled. His hands shook as it popped off and pills went everywhere. He picked up four, swallowed them, waved a hand in dismissal at the rest, and went back to bed. Shivering, he burrowed under his pile of blankets. Stared at the fire until his eyelids were heavy. He went under and didn't care if he came back up.

Sunlight stabbing his eyes pulled out a groan. He rolled over and tugged his blanket over his head and took stock: his head throbbed, mouth dry as cotton, throat a bit scratchy, but he was still here. He rolled over and covered his eyes with his arm and allowed himself to be still. He let the warmth of the sun seep in. But something jabbed at the back of his mind, sending a bolt of fear through him that had him flying out of bed, blanket tossed on the floor, feet kicking into motion, becoming a hurricane. "What day is it? What the hell day is it?" He muttered. He paced, raking his hand through his hair until a moment of inspiration struck. He flicked on the radio. Tapped his foot. Waited.

"Good morning, listeners. It's a beautiful start to our Monday. It looks like the cold is going to ease up its grip on us and give you a little break before the next big storm. If you're going to get out, this is the day. The sun is shining. It might even feel warm for those of us who are used to the North Country. Have a blessed day!"

Jesse sagged, one hand against the wall while he waited for his pulse rate to slow down. He hadn't missed his mom. Hadn't missed his supplies. Hadn't missed his Sunday visit with Stella. It had only been one night lost to a heavy sleep weighed down by a fever. Calmed, he went about his regular routine: coffee, hot and black, a bit of breakfast, some more ibuprofen for good measure, just in case anything was still brewing inside of him. He made up his bed, cleaned up, changed, thought about chopping more wood, but really didn't have any place to put it. *Still need to fill your rack indoors.* A shiver ran through him. He'd get to it in a bit.

He sat down with his second cup of coffee and sipped slowly, but something wouldn't let him settle. His mind took him back to his dream of Stella, and that had his insides going tight. Heat rushed to his temples, tempting him to go see her, check in on her, get close to her—

—longing to let her cure his loneliness.

He dressed in his warm gear, pulling a wool cap down over his ears and wrapping a scarf around his neck before plunging into the day. The cold sucked his breath away for only an instant. Once he got moving, heat pumped its way through him. He forewent snowshoes. He'd forged a path to the little house a mile away many times. Without fresh snow, he should be able to manage with ease. This journey, compared to all the rest in his life, was nothing. Birds sang while squirrels, rabbits, and chipmunks skittered about. They lifted his heart and pulled out a rusty whistle.

He made it to Stella's in good time. Smoke drifting from the chimney invited him in. He stomped his way up the deck steps to give her forewarning she had a visitor. He gave a hard rap on the door. No answer. He peered in the windows. No sign of her. His stomach clenched and his heart sank. He glanced down at the snow around his feet. Small footprints made a trail, moving away from the cabin. Heading into the wilderness. He cursed for the second time that morning. Where on earth had she gotten herself off to? Nothing for it but to look.

And pray the wilderness didn't swallow her whole.

Stella believed in being disciplined about her writing. She stuck to a routine every day. First thing in the morning, as soon as she woke up, she ran through her morning stretches, drank a cup of tea, ate fruit and oatmeal with a slice of multigrain toast. She sat down at the table by the window with her laptop and let the words flow from her fingers. There was only one problem. Every leading male character turned into someone who looked, sounded, and behaved exactly like the man on the mountain. Jesse didn't fit her Christmas novel or her deadline. But he was the only thing she thought about, day in and day out. The only thing she saw—

—whether her eyes were open or closed.

Frustrated, because any story with him in it was so much more irresistible than anything else she could write—*had* to write—she set her computer aside and threw back her quilt she'd been curled up in, perched in the comfy recliner by the fireplace that was soft enough to pull her in. Sit in it long enough and she'd be sound asleep. She had to get out, clear her head, get on track. Her agent and her publishing company expected her to come through. She glanced down at her pajamas. *Can't go out like this.* She pulled on her favorite jeans, a heavy sweater, and wool socks. She finished her preparations with the heavy boots, warm coat, hat, and gloves Jesse gave her. His gesture warmed her more than anything she could wear, filling her mind with his tormented eyes, strong jaw, broad back ready to bear the brunt of her problems and his. Spiking her pulse rate, raising her temperature, bringing her one step closer to the point of no return, to his doorstep—

—straight into his arms.

She took a few steps onto her porch, turning in the direction of her neighbor's snug little cabin. Common sense won out. "You don't know what you'll get yourself into if you go there right now. Best to turn yourself around, go back inside, and buckle down." She spoke out loud, an edge to her tone. Like it meant business.

Where's your sense of adventure? Her mother's voice propelled her on a new path she'd never tried before, headed toward the highest elevation of the mountain. Time to test her mettle. She took three steps, whacked herself on the forehead, and spun on her heel. She sprinted back inside. She filled her pocket with trail mix, fixed a thermos of hot tea, and hung her camera on her neck. On an impulse, she grabbed her journal and a pen to jot observations, hoping against hope to find inspiration. Sometimes, doing something completely unrelated to writing, something physical, started the creative juices flowing in her brain.

Legs pumping, arms swinging, sucking in deep breaths and pushing the air out in a cloud, Stella forged her way up, up, up and onward. A few times she had to pause, hands pressed to her knees, waiting for the stitch in her side to go away, to catch her breath. Her exercise DVDs didn't cut it when it came to preparing her for real exertion. Her legs ached more the higher she climbed, but it also felt invigorating to be outside, not just sitting alone inside that cabin. She wondered if coming to the mountains, tucked away in the woods, like something out of a fairy tale, had been the right decision. She hadn't made any progress in her Christmas story. Her heart kept taking over, telling her fingers to write about her mountain man.

Aggravated, she blew her bangs out of her eyes and took one step—the wrong step. The air whooshed out of her lungs as her body dropped into a crevice just wide enough for, oh say, an idiot writer. *Curiosity really did kill the cat.* At least she landed on her feet. She couldn't turn around, climb up or sit down. There wasn't any room to do anything except to stand. The rock walls pressed up against her on all sides, closing in. She closed her eyes. Counted to ten. Breathed in and out. Counted again. Forced herself to look up. She had to blink rapidly to clear her vision, face dusted with snow that had conveniently started falling. *Covering your tracks or any evidence you were ever here.* Her heart stuttered, skipped a beat, limped on. A ledge jutted out above her, some twenty feet or more in the air. She had no way of reaching it, no way of getting out. The only thing she could do was stand there and hope someone would come for her. Hikers were unlikely, not at this time of year, except for Jesse. Hope flickered inside her, warming her, only to be snuffed out seconds later. He wouldn't come to check in on her for several more days. A shiver ran through her from her head to her toes.

Heaven, help me.

He hunkered over the bar, milking the glass of a poor excuse for alcohol. Making it last. He'd slapped down his last dollar an hour ago and no one was offering drinks on the house. He didn't know where more money was coming from. A side hustle? Rough someone up in an alley? His mind looped in circles, considering his limited options. A small, wiry man in a dark coat with a ball cap pulled low over his eyes sat down next to him and nodded. Held up a finger to get the bartender's attention. He asked for a bourbon on the rocks in a gravelly voice. He laid money on the bar and gestured to his neighbor. "One for my friend, too."

"Friend?" He accepted the drink anyway, slugged it back, traced the scar running down his face out of habit. "Aren't you stretching it a bit, Sly?"

His benefactor's mouth drew up into a tight grin. "You took care of some nasty business for me. I always return a favor, J.C. You know it."

J.C. The name only a small circle of friends and enemies called him. He cleared his throat. "Did you find anything?"

Sly shook his head, swallowed his drink and tapped his finger on the bar for a refill. "Nothing. Not on either one of them."

J.C. went back to his first drink and took a gulp, breath hissing out. It stung going down. "Keep looking. I want that bastard. The woman can wait so I can make her suffer. She doesn't know what misery means. She's going to regret being born."

His companion nodded, slid him a sideways-glance, dark eyes glittering. "I'll have to dig deeper, crack my way into public records. It will take time."

J.C. shrugged. "I've got nothing but time."

And theirs is running out. If it's the last thing I do, they'll pay.

<h1 style="text-align:center">Chapter Six</h1>

Jesse eyed the tracks venturing off in the snow, away from his place or any place Stella might know. *"Ah, hell."* The thermometer said twenty degrees that morning when he woke up…and the temp was dropping. Judging by the ache in the arm and leg his father had broken, the best indicator of changes in the weather, a storm was coming. He reached down and gripped his sore thigh, reached across with his right hand to rub at his bicep. Gave it up for a lost cause. He nearly choked at the thought she'd gone wandering. *On her own!* He followed her tracks with ease, thankful it wasn't snowing, praying he'd find her sitting on a boulder, jotting in her notebook or talking to the squirrels. Until his hopes were dashed as her tracks veered off toward the peak of the mountain. A destination he'd climbed only once, soon after his arrival, before the snow flew.

It almost did him in.

His stomach flipped. *Please keep her safe.* He wasn't a praying man, but desperate times called for desperate measures. One hour ran into another. *How far did she go?* He cursed again, loudly and more vehemently, when the sky opened up and snow pelted down on him, erasing her tracks within minutes. He continued in what he hoped was the right direction, heart racing as the snow fell harder, and the skies grew darker. *Come on! Let me find her. I can't do this in the dark!* His heart hammered faster, picturing her alone, frightened or hurt, maybe worse, lying somewhere all night long.

He picked up his pace. Worried about her. That she may have collapsed, half frozen in the snow. God only knew how long she had been out. The temperature was plummeting. A much too vivid imagination, fueled by personal experiences of disaster, sent his panic level heading straight over the brink. But the girl surprised him. Her feet continued to move upward. Away from his cabin. Toward the unknown. Stella was tougher than he thought. Half an hour later, the path became more treacherous and his pulse raced. A fist of fear grabbed hold of his lungs and squeezed tight. She wasn't a seasoned hiker. She'd tire or get careless.

Jesse pushed faster, harder. He had to catch up with her. In such a rush, he didn't keep a close eye on the terrain. A slippery spot, ice hidden beneath the snow, sent him skittering down the slope. His body picked up momentum, propelling him to the bottom as his snowshoes flew off his boots. He landed flat on his back, the wind knocked out of him. He squeezed his eyes shut tight, huffing and puffing. Waiting to get past the terrifying feeling of not being able to breathe. His inner voice berated him with every gasp for air. *You can't afford to be careless! If you take yourself out, who's going to help Stella?*

Jesse wasted time he didn't have gathering up his snowshoes and strapping them back on as tightly as possible. He picked his way back up the mountain, carefully placing his steps to get traction, cursing the ice for slowing him down. He stopped for a moment, leaning on a boulder, and pushed on. A surge of adrenalin pushed him into a jog, lunging from one foot to the other, stretching his stride as far as it would go. A stitch stabbed deeply in his side as he pushed his breath between his teeth. He ignored it, ignored the chill setting in, the wind whipping right through him. He was really getting worried, calculating how long it would take to make it to town, bring in the cavalry if he didn't find her. *Too damn long!* Finally, he reached the peak. He walked in circles, gazed up, behind him, glanced over the edge, lump in his throat and heart tripping. His breath spilled out. No sign of her down there. He held on to a tree and waited for his feet to be steady. *All right. Here goes nothing.* He took a deep breath and bellowed at the top of his lungs, "*Stella!*"

Marlon Brando couldn't have done it better.

A muffled cry drifted his way. "Help! Can anyone hear me?"

He froze. "Stella! Where are you?" He held his breath, waiting for a response. Maybe he had imagined it.

"Oh my God. Down here! I'm down here!!" Her voice cracked. "I thought no one would ever come." The last was almost a whisper.

He turned slowly, carefully scanning his surroundings. He didn't want to take one wrong step and end up where she was. He inched forward and snow toppled over a narrow gap in the rocks. He cast a silent prayer up above. His wide snowshoe kept him from slipping through. He dropped down on his stomach and peered over the edge. A frightened gaze met his, her eyes nearly glowing in the dark, a brilliant splash of color against the dark shadows. Her face was white as a ghost, hat, hair, and eyebrows coated with snow. A sympathetic chill ran through him for her. "Are you hurt?"

"Does my pride count?" She grumbled through chattering teeth, managing a hint of a grin. "No, I'm not hurt. Just stuck."

"All right. Just hang in there. I'll get you out." He took off his snowshoes. He might need to dig in his toes, get some traction to pull her up. It looked like a twenty-foot drop. There was no way his arm would stretch. He had to find something to drop down to her. *Note to self: from now on, carry a pack with essentials, including a rope.* A few Our Fathers and Hail Mary's weren't out of the question, but this moment called for action.

A shiver ran through him, a debilitating fear creeping in. What if he *couldn't* help her? His unease kicked it up a notch as a chill shook him. The temperature had dropped considerably in the time it took him to trek up the mountain. He glanced up at the skies and cursed under his breath. The clouds had darkened and were hugging the horizon. *Big storm coming in. What has fallen is nothing.* He had no time to lose. He spun around, checked his surroundings, and found nothing that could pull anything as substantial as a girl from a crevice deep in the earth that had tried to swallow her up.

She had one thing in her favor. The temperature would hold steady down there, like in a cave. *Hopefully* she wouldn't freeze to death. A chill shook him again. Jesse couldn't predict the same for himself which would put her back in the same predicament. Stuck in a crevice with no way out, no one aware of her location, and no one to rescue her. He was her only chance. *Don't screw up!* He viciously shut down the angry voice in his head from the monster that told him all his life how utterly useless he was.

"Hello? Jesse? Are you still up there?" The tremor in her voice made him want to tuck her in close, keep her safe. "Jesse…I don't know how much longer I can take it down here. I'm really cold and it's so small. I can't breathe."

He dropped on his stomach once more to gaze down at her, forcing his lips to quirk up in the corners in what he hoped gave him a devil may care expression. "Sweetheart, I'm not going anywhere. I'll get you out. Just give me a moment. And listen. You *can* breathe. Close your eyes. I'll count to five. Breathe in. Now let it out." She stopped gasping even though her face looked pale enough to glow in the darkness.

He pushed back on his heels and pressed his hands to his temples, eyes closed tight but he couldn't erase her gaze burning through his shields or any illusions. *Think! Think! Think! You need a rope. Like Rapunzel.* He tapped himself on the temple a little harder than he'd intended. *A rope! Exactly what you need!* He unzipped his coat and whipped it off, pulling out his pocketknife. Taking off the arms, then more sections, knotting them together. He stretched out on his belly, wincing at the tears glistening on Stella's cheeks. She hadn't complained or made a sound, but her eyes spoke volumes. Shakespeare couldn't have said that much in one of his tragic plays if he tried. "I'm tossing this down. Grab hold and I'll pull you up." He heaved the remnants of his coat over the edge. The cable dangled in front of her—

—falling short of its destination by about five feet.

She gave it her best shot, jumping as high as she could, grunting in frustration with the effort. "It's no use. I'm too short. I've always wondered why I couldn't have been tall like my father."

"It's all right. Let me make an adjustment." He pulled up the makeshift rope, tugged his sweater over his head, and shredded it next. He tied the heavy yarn on one end and knotted it extra tight before lobbing it down to her. Praying all the while. This time, it made it. His heart slowed to its normal rhythm, coming down out of the danger zone. "Grab it and hold on tight." As soon as a hearty tug pulled at him, he shouted, "Are you ready?"

"It's now or never." Her voice bounced off the rock walls and echoed as she stared up at him. She jerked her head in a nod. Whatever fear she'd shown before had been squashed down. Out of sight. He had to admire her. The girl had grit.

He backed up, slipping and sliding in the snow, dropping to his knees. Snow soaked through his worn jeans. The wind blasted the mountain, making a mournful howl, a sheet of snow coming down on him with the full force of nature. The cold seeped into his bones, latching on, sinking its teeth in. He ignored it, clamped his jaw shut to take control of his chattering teeth, strained his muscles for all he was worth, and pulled, hand over hand. Finally, her head poked up over the edge. He lunged forward, landing on his chest, *oomph,* and gripped her hand. "I've got you." He brought her all the way up and fell back, lying flat, gazing up at the sky, gasping for breath.

She leaned against him, her eyes closed. Her warmth took off a bit of the chill. Her head rested on his shoulder. "Thank you. Thank you so much." Her eyelids sprang wide, forehead creased. "Look at you! You've got nothing on!" She glanced at the rope in her hands. "Oh my God! It's your coat and sweater! You're going to get frostbite! What were you thinking?"

"I was thinking about keeping you alive." He met her gaze, his voice low. He stood up quickly. "The cold can't catch me if we get moving. Let's book it before this storm gets any worse and we can't find our way back."

As it was, it took at least two hours to work their way back down the mountain, Jesse holding his snowshoes with one arm. It was too hard to keep in step with her unless they both walked in boots. Her snowshoes broke in the fall. The temperature dipped lower, the snow getting heavier, slowing them down. Whiteout conditions cut visibility down, blotting out the trail and any landmarks that he'd mapped out to navigate the wilderness that enveloped his cabin. The cold set into his bones. He started limping. His leg, the one that took the brunt of his monster's fury, hurt like a bastard in weather like this. Stella noticed, ducking under his arm to give him extra support. He had to hand it to her. She was made of tough stuff. They went to his place because it was closer. He'd never been so happy in his life to see the place he called home.

Welcoming him for a change.

Jesse was running on empty when they reached his front steps. His teeth chattered so hard he thought they'd break, the shivers running through him almost to the point of convulsions. Stella wrapped an arm around his waist as he stumbled up his steps. "Come on now. Keep going. Almost there. Put one foot in front of the other. That's it." They burst through the door. She slammed it shut behind them and locked it for good measure, leaning against it for a few seconds to catch her breath.

He dropped to his knees and collapsed on the floor with a blast of cold air rushing in after them. *Should get up, build up the fire, get more wood.* Everything went black. He came to, still lying on the floor but covered in blanket, his wet socks peeled off. The wood snapped and crackled. Stella had managed to get the fire going. She touched his forehead. "You need to get in a warm shower. You may have hypothermia. Let me help you."

For once he didn't argue. *Too cold.* She leaned down, allowing him to hook his arm over her shoulders, and they came up together. Side by side, they staggered to the shower. She propped him on the toilet as she turned on the water. He balked at her helping him to strip down to nothing.

"Oh stop. I took care of my grandfather when he lived with us. Don't flatter yourself. There isn't anything I haven't seen." He had no choice at this point, too weak to barely stand. She worked at his clothes in concentration as they fought her, lip pinned between her teeth, eyebrows knit together. She looked up and her eyes went wide, a gasp slipping out. Her fingers skimmed over the damage his father had left behind: a mean, jagged scar on his upper arm; another running down his upper thigh; burn marks, thin lines—a roadmap of pain and suffering. She clamped her mouth shut and got him in the shower, grabbed pajamas, and led him to the chair by the fire after he'd spent ten minutes under a rush of hot water, covering him in a thick comforter. Finally, she dropped beside him on her knees, and took his hand, her eyes bright with unshed tears. "What happened to you?"

"My father happened to me. He gave me compound fractures in my left arm and leg the day he threw me down the stairs when I was nine. He told the emergency room doctors I'd had a nasty fall, even managed to squeeze out some crocodile tears." One hand kneaded at his thigh. It hurt every day since, some days more than others. His other hand skimmed over the angry red circle with a dark center on his left shoulder. "This is where he burned me…with the cigarette lighter in the car…because I had to go to the bathroom, when I was four. Believe me. I went to the bathroom. From that day forward, I stopped drinking if we were going for a drive."

Stella flinched, her fingers tightening their grip on him. "Didn't anyone ever try to help? I know how hard it must have been for your mother. Abused women feel powerless, but what about neighbors? Your pediatrician? Teachers? Anyone?"

He shook his head. "The bastard was smart. He targeted spots no one would see and put the fear of God into me if I ever told." Jesse laughed without humor. "I finally got lucky, though; you saw the web of lines all over my body? The monster did them with his jackknife, just enough to make me bleed. To make me pay for being born at all. I was twelve years old, in the sixth grade, changing my clothes in the locker room at school when the gym teacher saw some of the fresh cuts. He called Child Protective Services. They came to the house, turned up the heat. That's when my old man stopped picking on me—physically. It didn't stop him from taking his anger out on my mom because she wouldn't talk. Ever. Not as long as he promised not to hurt her boy anymore. She didn't know that hurt me so much worse, all the times he went after her. I hid in my room, but I couldn't block out the thumps of him hitting her, her crying—the screaming." He covered his ears. "God, I still hear it!"

She climbed onto the chair beside him and wrapped her arms around him, pulling him close, giving him her warmth and a soft place to land. "Shh. You're all right. That was a long time ago. It's over now."

"It will never be over," he choked out the words raggedly. They sat in silence, listening to the woodstove, the wind buffeting the cabin, moaning eerily like a ghost. He inhaled a stuttering breath. "I came here to put it all behind me, but it always catches up with me." His fist came down hard on the arm of the chair. "*Dammit!* Can't something go right today?"

"You saved me. I'd say that went right." Stella's voice was soft, her fingers trailing through his hair, over and over, gently, so gently.

His eyelids drooped, so heavy he couldn't hold them up. A moan slipped out. "That feels *so good*. I can't remember the last time someone touched me this way." He leaned in closer, and a tremor ran through his body. "I'm still cold. *So cold*."

"Well, I'll warm you up the best that I can." She flitted away, returning with thick, wool socks. "Let's get these on." When his hands shook so hard he kept dropping them, she helped without making a to-do about it. She tucked the blanket around him tight enough to make him feel like a mummy. "I'll be right back." His head fell back as he dozed in and out. Minutes later, she returned with a steaming cup of tea, waking him with a jerk. "Drink this right now. You need to get yourself warmed up on the inside, too." Dutifully, he drank it. She set the cup down on the table beside the chair, wincing as his blanket trembled. "I don't think it worked."

"I just can't stop shaking and I'm so…so cold. It's like I'm turning to ice." He wrapped his arms around his chest, tucking his hands beneath his armpits. Trying to find a scrap of heat anywhere in his body.

Without missing a beat, she lifted the blanket and slipped under it, pressing her body flush against his, wrapping her arms and legs around him. "My mama always told me I was like a heater when we would cuddle together while she read bedtime stories to me. Let me thaw you out." She moved in closer, much closer, and he could climb under her skin.

He could live with that.

He buried his head in the crook of her neck. Inhaled. Spoke hoarsely. "I hear skin on skin is what you're really supposed to do to keep from freezing to death."

She chuckled softly, nudging him in the ribs. "Don't push your luck, buddy."

He let his eyes droop, and his body went loose as she worked her magic on him. Gradually, her heat traveled through him, from head to toe. A distant memory that he'd locked away, deep in the back of his mind with all the snippets of anything good or happy, brought him back to a time when all was right in his world. To the most important woman in his life who gave *him* life, loved him with all her heart, and he felt safe.

Maybe Stella would be the woman he could call home.

"No! No! Leave her alone, you bastard! Leave her alone!" Jesse's shout, ragged and raw, ripped through the darkness. He thrashed so hard he sent Stella sprawling on the floor with a thump.

Half awake, the world spinning out of control, giving her a hint of what vertigo felt like, she scrambled up on her knees and shook his shoulder. "Hey, hey! It's just a dream! Wake up!" She backed away as his arm flailed. The heat of the woodstove was so hot she dodged to the side, afraid of getting singed—too close for comfort. Smacking against it would have meant a nasty burn. Jesse's agonized groan hit her hard in the gut. Heedless of her own safety, she flung herself at him and wrapped her arms around him as tightly as she could. "You're okay! It's just a dream. He isn't here. He can't hurt you. Won't hurt you ever again." She kissed his hair like a mother would comfort her child. "No one's here."

His body suddenly went still. "You are." His voice drifted into the darkness, small, vulnerable and filled with pain, slipped inside her, wrapped around her heart. She ached for him, wanted to take away all his suffering, fix him like she would with a flurry of her fingertips running over her keys in a story. But this wasn't a story. This was real. She grazed his forehead with a kiss.

He scalded her with the touch of his skin.

"You're burning up!" She threw back the blanket and dashed to the kitchen, wet a towel with cold water, and hurried back. She wet his wrists and the back of his neck. She quickly folded the towel and set it on his forehead. "Do you have any medicine? We've got to bring your fever down."

His eyes drooped shut, one hand rising slowly into the air. "It's in…the bathroom…medicine cabinet."

She sprinted out of the room, mouth dry, heart banging against her ribs. Seconds later, she returned with a glass of water and a bottle of pills that slipped out of her hands. The heat rolled off him, hot enough to make *her* sweat, and he was shaking so hard he produced a personal earthquake, the blankets quivering. The vibrations traveled through her. She ignored the pills that scattered on the floor. There would be time to get them later. She snatched up three and placed them in his hand. She had to hold the glass his hands were shaking so badly. Even so, water sloshed all over him as he gulped a few swallows to wash down the pills. "Drink it, all of it before you get dehydrated." She set the glass aside when the water was all gone and ran her fingers through his hair. "You're sick. You need to try and rest now. Sleep could be the best medicine for you right now. You've been pushing yourself too hard."

"Mmm." A hint of a smile bloomed as he leaned into her touch. "My…my mother used to…stroke my hair when I was…." His words trailed off and sleep pulled him under before she could say anything.

Wide awake, she sat perched on the edge of his recliner, staring at him, watching his chest rise and fall, willing his temperature to come down into a safe zone. She laid her palm on his forehead from time to time, giving him the reassurance of a comforting touch—something she knew had been lacking in his life. Touching him only spiked her level of panic. Anxiety sent her thoughts racing faster and faster, running in circles, bringing her back to where she started— with a tortured young man, who was practically a stranger, stealing her heart.

Daylight slipped in through the curtains, bringing no relief. Jesse's body was still a furnace. If he didn't cool off soon, the fever could do serious damage. She had to find a way to bring down his temperature. Carry in some snow or drag him outside to bury him in it. Pent up energy propelled her to her feet. She walked from one end of the room to the other, back and forth. Back and forth. She built up the woodstove, throwing on more logs. The room was so warm, sweat ran off her in rivulets. But not him. The fever *had* to break!

She paced. Paced. Paced. What if he was in real trouble? How long would it take for soaring temperatures to fry the human brain? She thought of the flood of medical dramas she'd binged, considered all her novels. There had to be at least one example of someone who was dangerously ill. Stella couldn't think of one now, only knew she was sorely unprepared for emergencies. No phone. No other people knew where she was except for the owner of her rental cabin, and they wouldn't come checking in on the place until after Christmas or whenever someone new was supposed to check in, and Stella booked it an extra month in case she didn't want to leave. *Brilliant, girl. Just brilliant. What if you really were in trouble all by yourself? They'd find your bones like Chris McCandless!*

She tapped her fingers on the edge of a table. Wracking her brain for a solution. There was nothing for it. She'd have to trek miles down the trail to get to her car. She ran to the window, glanced out, and pressed her hands against the cold glass. "Of course! It's snowing again!" Her car wouldn't get through several feet of snow. Besides, how on earth could she get a full-grown man down the mountain all by herself? And walk to town on her own? She wasn't even sure which way to go! *He just must get better!* She went back to his side, placed her hand on his forehead and yanked it back, practically scorched. The heat was pouring off him.

Four more hours dragged by, four of the longest hours of her life, while she walked the perimeter of the room, willing him to get well, help to come, or time to stop. She changed cold cloths on his forehead as soon as they became warm to the touch. Which only took a few minutes. She was amazed that his skin wasn't sizzling; it was so hot, singeing her finger when she grazed him, through his shirt with layers of blankets heaped on top of him. She held his hand when the shaking started. His face twisted, his breathing coming harder. Unable to stand seeing him in pain, she retreated to the window and gazed out at the snow piling up.

When the shaking hit him so hard he tumbled out of his chair and hit the floor with a loud thud, she couldn't take it anymore. She pulled on her boots and a coat, grabbed his arms, and started tugging on him. When he hardly budged, she grabbed a quilt, shimmied him on to it, and kept going, grunting and panting as she made agonizingly slow progress. Inching slowly across the room, ready to sob in frustration, she flung the door open. Buffeted by the wind—it almost pushed her back inside—but there was no stopping her now. Snow sprinkled her hair, coating her eyelashes. She blinked hard and fast, fighting tears so she could see. Fiercely praying. *Please. Please, God, be with him. Help him. Please. Help me help him.* She pulled with all her might, a scream rising out of her throat as she did, and dragged him down the steps, into the deep snow. She threw it on top of him, burying him like a kid in the sand at the beach. Covering his entire body and layering a blanket of snow on top of him. She cupped his face in her hands. "Wake up! Jesse! It's Stella! You've *got* to wake up!"

She glanced over her shoulder. This had to work. There was no way she could drag him all the way down the mountain to her car.

And even if she did, they'd be snowed in.

"Oh…my…God! I'm…fr…fr…freezing!" Her living snowman's stutter yanked her back from the brink of a panic attack. She caught his hands as he floundered in the snow, trying to burrow his way out.

"You've been burning up with a terrible fever. I had to get you cooled off." She started digging to reach him, hands moving fast and furiously. "I had to do something to bring your temperature down. Nothing else would work." She grabbed hold of his hand. "Come on. Let's get back inside before you freeze to death."

He rose to his feet and staggered from side to side. She flung his arm around her shoulders. Slowly they made their way back into the house. Stella slammed the door shut, and they both leaned against it, gasping for breath. Jesse jerked his chin toward the small couch against the wall. "I really need to lie back down or I'm going to fall right here where I stand, and I don't think I can make it to my bed."

"First, you need to get out of those wet clothes." She reached for his shirt.

He held up his hand. "I can manage." He swayed where he stood while she stared at him. "A little privacy, please."

"Don't be ridiculous! I helped you before. You're about to drop." Stella turned around when he gave her a glare that could set the cabin on fire. She stood with her hands on her hips, tapping her foot, waiting for the rustling of the covers, before turning around to see him buried in blankets on the sofa that was more like a loveseat. "You're still shaking. Really hard. I'll get you some warm clothes."

"No." He shook his head, his hand snagging her shirt. "Please. Please don't leave me alone. I don't want to be alone anymore."

She sat down on the arm of the couch, pulling another blanket off the back. Her fingers gently trailed through his hair again. "I'm not going anywhere. Promise." *Couldn't if I tried.* Slowly, the shivering stopped. She looked down. His eyes were trained on the woodstove. A tear trickled down his cheek. She gently wiped it away. "Who left you alone?"

"My mother." He shook his head. "She didn't have a choice. The monster kept her away from me. He hurt her. Always hurt her." He mumbled, his voice dipping low as his eyes drooped.

"And that hurt you worse than anything *he* ever did to you." She let her palm rest on the crown of his head. He didn't answer, the tides of sleep too heavy for him to resist. But at least he was cool. She slid down on the floor and propped her head against the couch. She pressed against his leg, sharing her warmth. Questions crowded her mind. One ranked at the top of the list.

Where was his monster now?

Chapter Seven

The door of the ramshackle house slammed hard enough to shake the walls and rattle the windows, louder than a hurricane. Jesse expected it to collapse with one good huff and puff from his monster, worse than the Big Bad Wolf could ever be. He hunkered down under his threadbare covers, shivering with fear and a chill. The heat had been shut off *again*. He pulled his pillow over his head, trying desperately to make himself smaller. Invisible. It never worked. He could never get small enough.

Footsteps stomped through the house, heavy and echoing like the giant in *Jack and the Beanstalk* Mama had read to him at bedtime. A low growl raised the hair on the back of Jesse's neck. He tucked himself into a tighter ball against the headboard, wishing he could disappear or walk into his closet and end up in Narnia, another story Mama read to him when his father wasn't home. "Where's my dinner? A man ought to have dinner on the table when he walks in the door!" Something banged on the table. His fist? "Give me my dinner, woman! Right now!"

"It's midnight, John. I didn't think you were coming home. You didn't call." His mother's timid, barely audible voice, soft enough to be a whisper, still made it past her son's fortress of blankets, piercing right through him. Painful enough to stab his heart.

Jesse gripped the cross underneath his pajama shirt, eyes squeezed shut tightly and prayed fervently. *Please don't hurt her. Please don't hurt her. Please don't hurt her!*

"Don't you sass me, woman!" His monster's voice spiked into a full-blown roar. Something crashed against the wall then thumped on the floor. Quiet whimpering made the boy's eyes sting. "Now get in that kitchen and make me something to eat, woman, *now*, or I'll really give you something to cry about!"

The pitter-pat of light footsteps scurried toward the kitchen, his father's steel-toed boots thundering after her. Pots and pans clanged on the stove, cabinets creaked, the refrigerator door whooshed open and clicked shut. The soft murmur of his mother's voice was too quiet to hear. The thudding of Jesse's heart in his ears died down. Maybe, just maybe, his mother could hold off the storm tonight; give his monster a beer; sing him to sleep; cast a spell so he'd never wake up—

—just like a fairytale.

The kitchen chair scraped across the floor, and another bang on the table made Jesse jerk. "What's taking you so long, and where's my beer?" Something pinged off the wall. Some loud glugging, a burp, and a mean laugh traveled down the hallway, slipping into the little boy's room and taunting him. "That's more like it." Silverware clinked on the table. His father grunted like an animal. "Give me that leftover meatloaf from last night's dinner, woman."

"That's...that's all there is, Don. We had the rest...for our dinner." Her voice got smaller, quieter. Jesse pictured her trying to shrink too. A loud smack rang out followed by his mother's cry. He bit his lip to keep from calling out. He was too little. He couldn't help her. Couldn't help himself. Maybe he really was useless—

—like his monster said.

"I bet you gave it all to the boy, didn't you? Always giving it to the boy!" The footsteps thundered in the hallway as they approached Jesse's bedroom.

"Leave him alone, John! He has to eat too! He's just a little tyke. He's smaller than the rest of the kids in his class as it is!" The door creaked loudly as the footsteps came closer, and still his mother tried to stop a force as strong as a wrecking ball. *"Don't hurt him!"*

Another smack rang out and something crashed against the wall. A hush fell over the room. Jesse's mouth went dry. His heart tripped. He hunkered down, pressing his back against the wall, trying to become one with the wood. A second later, he dove off the side of the bed just as his father ripped off the covers. Jesse scrambled around his father, past his mother, unconscious on the floor, her mouth bleeding, down the hallway toward the back door. His hand grabbed hold of the knob as the footsteps came after him.

Hot breath brushed his neck, reeking of alcohol, the terrible smell smothering him. A cloud of cigarette smoke in his father's clothes making him cough as a big, rough hand gripped the collar of his shirt, choking him as he was hoisted into the air. His feet kicked frantically, trying to get away, like a fish on a hook, hands grabbing arms that were much too strong. "Just where do you think you're going?" The glowering face and figure looming in front of him proved there weren't any monsters under his bed. Jesse would take them any day. His monster was very real, bloodshot eyes terrifying the little boy. He saw them in his sleep—

—if he could sleep.

His father's eyes shot open wide as a blur slammed into his knees, taking him down to the floor. "I told you to leave him alone!" His mother pulled Jesse away. She got to her feet and ran to the kitchen, grabbed the frying pan off the stove, and whipped it at her husband, hitting him in the head.

It didn't stop him, only made him as mad as a bear. He grabbed her by her hair, yanked it, and smashed her head against the wall. Jesse's face scrunched up as he howled. "Mama!" He raised his little five-year-old hands in fists and threw himself at his father, pummeling him as hard as he could. "You stop being mean to my mama!"

His father's eyes glowed with an evil light, and he leered at Jesse. "Go ahead. Keep hitting me. Give me your best shot. Someone's got to teach you how to be a man. It won't be that mousy little mother of yours." When Jesse exhausted himself, sobbing, his hands falling to his sides, his father nodded. "Now it's my turn." He grabbed hold of his son like he was a ball and flung him against the wall. The little boy slumped in a heap on the floor, blood trickling from a gash on the back of his head. His father's steel-toed boot kicked him for good measure.

"Stop it, you bastard! Leave me the hell alone!" Jesse shot up, panting, hair plastered to his head, clothes damp with sweat. The warmth of the woodstove hit him like a wall of heat, pushing him back against the pillows.

A gentle hand took his and held on tight. "No one's going to hurt you. You've been sick."

For a moment, he thought it was his mother sitting beside him, her voice soft and comforting. He squeezed his eyes shut, looked again. He recognized his neighbor, realizing she was more than a neighbor. She was a friend. The girl had to be a friend to take care of him the way she had. He sagged against the cushions and met Stella's gaze. She had shadows in her eyes, her face pinched. He must not have made it easy on her. He swallowed hard. "I'm sorry. I was having a nightmare."

"Fevers will do that." Her palm, gentle and warm, touched his forehead. She sighed. "Thank goodness. I think yours has finally broken. You've been sick for two days. I was getting ready to forge a path through the snow into town if the snow bath didn't work."

His eyebrows shot up. "Snow bath?" He glanced at the distance to the front door, pictured the flight of steps, and eyed her up and down. "You're a lot tougher than you look."

She shrugged. "I did what I had to do when I didn't have any other choice. I know you would too." She stood up. "Let me get you some tea." She brought back two cups; she'd kept a kettle warm on the top of the woodstove. "Drink the whole thing. It has extra milk and sugar. You need it. You've got to be awfully weak." She slowly sipped at hers and waited until his was almost gone. "You cried out about your monster."

Silence fell between them, the crackling of the wood in the fire the only sound. He stared at the flames, lost in the dance of light and shadows. He wondered if the fire in his heart, the anger, would ever die out. Thought about lying but reconsidered. He'd held this inside all his life. Only talked to his mother about the skeleton in his closet. Maybe talking about it with Stella would help. "I can't seem to escape him, but don't worry. My father won't be hurting anyone anymore. I made sure of it."

She didn't bat an eye, sipping at her tea casually—too casually—as if she didn't care about what he just said. Her back, ramrod straight, taut jaw, and white knuckles said otherwise. "What do you mean you made sure of it?"

He didn't like the hint of fear in her voice hidden in a tremor. He set down his cup and met her gaze . Kept his voice steady. "I didn't kill him if that's what you're thinking." He pushed his breath out between his teeth. "But I made sure the last time he hurt my mother was *the last time.*"

Her face softened. "He abused both of you." A sure statement. Not a question.

He winced, tipped his head down, studied the blanket covering him. "It's something that's scarred me. Something I'll carry with me for the rest of my life."

"That's why you ended up here. This is your fresh start." Strangely enough, her posture loosened. Her mouth quirked up at the corners. "Why are you staring at me like that?"

"I can't believe you're not running away from me as fast as you can." A lingering shiver ran through him.

She grabbed his hand. "I'm not going anywhere. If I haven't run away yet, I'm not going to start now." She leaned in close, cupped his face in her palm. "I've spent enough time with you to know what kind of person you are."

"You hardly know me." His eyebrows knit together.

"I know enough." She leaned in closer, her breath kissing his skin. "Your actions speak much louder than words. If you did something to your father, you had no choice."

He stared at her and moved in closer. "What are my actions saying now?" She leaned in and pressed her lips to his. "That wasn't an answer."

"I guess *my* actions speak louder than words." Her whisper slipped in his ear and wrapped around him, drawing him against her until he fell into her—

—home sweet home.

Stella rolled onto her back, gaze pinned to the ceiling, trying to pierce the darkness. Her breath came out in a huff, lifting her bangs from her forehead. Her body was tight. She ought to be exhausted with all the stress of taking care of Jesse, staying up to watch him, pace, worry, drag him outside and back. She ought to be dead to the world. Instead, she couldn't even close her eyes.

It was like an electric current pulsed through her.

The mere presence of the man on the couch in the next room was all-consuming, pushing all other thoughts out of her head. He'd insisted she take his bed, that as soon as he was well enough, he'd escort her back to her place. He didn't want her to try and go by herself, not with a storm blasting them full-force, winds howling outside, shaking the little cabin, the snow mounting at an alarming pace. She'd pulled on her boots, coat, hat and gloves with the best of intentions: to shovel the deck, the steps, a path to the wood pile. His firm touch on her shoulder told her otherwise, turning her back to face him. His eyes still bright, a little warm, the fever rearing its head, face scruffy with stubble. He was even more ruggedly handsome. Why couldn't she remember how to breathe?

"You're not going out there. It's late and the snow isn't stopping. It can wait until morning." He wilted, pressing one palm on the closed door. The trip across the room had taken a toll on him.

Stella ducked under his shoulder and helped him back to his makeshift bed on the couch by the fire. She pulled up the covers, tossed a few logs in the woodstove, came back and pressed a palm to his forehead. She shook her head. "You're warm again." She went to the kitchen for water and a few more aspirins. "No more getting up. And as for shoveling, what if we need to get out of here?"

He took the pills dutifully and gulped a few swallows. He leaned back against his pillow, one eyebrow raised, expression playful. "And how are you getting me down the mountain anyway?"

She crossed her arms. "Who said anything about getting *you* down? I'd have to break a trail and come back for you."

"Sure, sure. You talk a good game." His mouth curved in a slip of a smile as his eyes drooped. He was fading. Still, his hand reached out, found hers, fingers curling around hers. "You couldn't leave me." His head tipped to the side, his soft snoring comforting.

She leaned in and lightly grazed his forehead with her lips. "You're right. Not a chance."

She'd set the cabin to rights: washed dishes, built up the woodstove so it wouldn't need anything until morning, and blew out the oil lamps. She checked her patient one last time, reassured he was cool again.

Which is what brought her to where she was now. Staring at the ceiling. Watching the play of shadows and moonlight on the wall. Longing to go out to the next room , to wrap her body around his and see if it felt as good as it looked, if he was a furnace all the time, if he truly was the perfect model for her next novel.

She snorted and whispered to herself, "Next novel? Quit lying to yourself. He's taken over everything you've tried to write since the day you met him."

A quiet tapping on her door startled her. "Stella, are you all right? I heard talking."

"I'm fine. Just working out a story idea. I usually use a notebook." She slipped out of bed and hurried to the door to pull it open. He stood with one arm braced against the jamb, swaying slightly. She bit her lip. "You need to lie down before you collapse." She pointed to the bed. "*Now.*"

Something in her tone or her eyes kept him from arguing. He stretched out on his bed with a sigh and patted the side next to him. "Plenty of room. Be a shame to waste it. I promise I won't take advantage of you." He winked. "Couldn't if I wanted to."

She thought about putting on his flannel shirt, another pair of pajama bottoms. Socks. Maybe his coat. She shook her head. *Don't be ridiculous! He's not going to do anything to you!* She scooted in next to him and pulled up the covers.

He slid closer, tucking her in against him. A slight shiver ran through him. She pushed herself closer, lending him any heat she had. He nodded. "There. It's not so bad. Is it?" She could hear the smile in his voice.

"No. It's not so bad. Go to sleep now. You need it." Not so bad? It only set her heart to racing, her mercury level rising toward the danger zone. Any hotter and she'd be a human torch. She couldn't believe he didn't notice. Until a slight tapping of his fingers on the covers in time with her heartbeat told her otherwise.

His breath kissed her cheek. "I feel it, too. It's just not the time. Yet. Let me catch my breath, get my strength back."

She knew the moment he fell asleep when his body went loose. She enjoyed his solid warmth and let herself sink into pleasant dreams, each one led her back to the darkhaired, blue-eyed man. When she woke up in the morning, the bed was empty, the sun shining brightly. A chipper whistling brought her to the kitchen. Jesse was whipping up an omelet. One look at her and he lit up like the Fourth of July. "You're awake! I was beginning to wonder if you'd fallen under a spell." He handed her a coffee cup. "Light and sweet, just the way you like it."

She took a sip, smiled. "It really is good. Thank you." She surveyed him up and down. "You seem much better this morning."

"Must have been my nurse." He winked and set a steaming plate in front of her. He settled in a chair across from her with his own plate.

"It was the least I could do for my bold and brave rescuer." They ate in companionable silence, the morning sunshine bringing a flood of relief with it. A crisis had been averted. Stella could relax for the first time since nearly getting swallowed up by a huge crack in the mountain.

"So, now it's my turn to help you." His fingers entwined with hers on the table and she almost dropped her cup. "What drove a successful woman like you up a mountain to a cabin in the middle of nowhere?"

Chapter Eight

Stella jumped up so fast the chair fell over with a bang. "I don't want to talk about it!" She walked as far away as she could to the small window overlooking the backyard, cursing the cabin for being so damn small. The walls closed in on her until she fought to breathe. Everything cozy about the cabin transformed into a trap. She stomped her foot. It was snowing, *again*—

—which meant no way out.

A chair scraped slowly across the floor behind her. Slow, measured footsteps came her way, giving her plenty of warning so she wouldn't get spooked. A warm, firm hand rested gently on the nape of her neck and kneaded at the tense muscles running from one shoulder to the other. "It's all right. I know. It's hard baring your soul. If you're not ready, I'm not going to push it. Your business is your business. But if you ever do want to talk, I'm a good listener."

An image filled her mind: a little boy curled up in bed with his mother, hugging her with everything he had in him while she cried, dabbing at a black eye, brokenly telling her son his daddy hit her. Stella ran her finger across her eyes, wiping away tears, and turned to face

Jesse. Stepping in when he opened his arms. Leaning her head on the sturdy, flannel-covered wall of his chest. His heartbeat was reassuringly strong and steady as she pressed her ear against his body. She let out a sniffle and whispered, "My mama died while I was away doing a book signing. I hurried to the hospital as soon as I got word she had a heart attack, but I was too late. I didn't get to say goodbye." She let out a shuddering breath. "I haven't been able to write since. Not really. I should have been there!" A sob broke loose, shaking her.

"Sweetheart, I've learned life doesn't usually happen the way we want it to." He knelt down, his arm coming under her legs, and scooped her up like a cradle. He carried her over to the chair by the woodstove and sat down. He held her, stroking the hair from her eyes. "You thought coming here would fix that." She nodded. He sat quietly, listening to the wood pop and crackle in the fireplace. "How long do you have to get your work done?"

"I need to do a radio broadcast on Christmas Eve with the rest of the novel submitted to my publisher that night by midnight." Her hands clenched together, knuckles turning white, as a tear trickled down her cheek. "I'm *not* going to meet the deadline. My publisher will drop me!"

He pressed a finger under her chin, lifting her head up until her gaze met his. "No more talk like that, you hear? You just need to take a deep breath, clear your mind, and find your center. Maybe this will help." He leaned in and grazed her lips with his.

Electricity sizzled through her body, like she had been shocked, and the floor tilted. Her fingers clenched around his shoulders, reeling him in, sealing his mouth with hers until necessity forced them to come up for air. She touched her lips with trembling fingers, a giggle slipping out. "That was definitely a good distraction."

He grinned. "Maybe we should try it again." His fingers threaded through her hair, cupping the back of her head, his grip firm as he came in for one more kiss. Good thing he was holding on or she would fall to the floor.

Stella stood back while he built up the fire in her fireplace, checked her supplies, hung up her coat and set her boots against the wall. "You know I can do all those things. I am a full-grown, capable woman."

Jesse rubbed his hands together with a chuckle. "I know you are very capable…of many things. Anyone who could manage to drag me outside, cover me in snow, and drag me back has my admiration and utmost respect. I just wanted to make sure you're all set. My way of saying thank you for taking such good care of me."

"I think you've had practice at taking care of people." She stepped in and kissed his cheek, then his lips, leaving him lightheaded. The room even spun a little. His hands clasped her elbows to steady himself. "You're sure you don't want to stay for dinner?"

Dinner? How about forever? He pushed the thought out of his mind and stepped back. He had to distance himself from her or he wouldn't be able to leave. "Thank you, but I need to let you get back to your writing. I have a feeling your fingers are going to be flying." He tapped his head. "Plenty of food for thought, right?" He reeled her in for one more hug and a hasty kiss before opening the door. If he lingered on her lips for too long, he'd be intoxicated. "Pop over any time you need to bounce off some ideas or just need a break. Otherwise, I'll be by in a week to make sure you're alright. Someone needs to keep you in the land of the living with real people. Have a good night, Stella."

"You too, Jesse. Sweet dreams. Mine will be all about you." Her voice, filled with longing and light, lit a flame in his chest that kept him warm all the way home. It flickered in his mind as he ate a bowl of soup, built up the fire in the woodstove, and crawled into bed. A long sigh slipped out.

He wished his bed wasn't empty.

He rolled from side to side, pounded his pillow,

twisted his blankets all around his body with his tossing and turning. Staring at the ceiling, his mind stuck replaying his childhood, his father, his mother, what his monster did to her. Thinking about what he wanted to do to his old man, what he already did. Heaven, help him, it wasn't enough. It would never be enough.

Until his monster was dead.

And to top it off, that sweet little thing up the mountain crowded out all other thoughts. *Stella.* Jesse couldn't get her out of his head. And the more he thought about her, the more it stoked the coals burning deep inside of him. For her. Until an inferno coursed through his blood. Unable to lie still another instant, he threw back the covers. Pulled on a pair of jeans, a flannel shirt, socks, and boots. Tugged on his coat even though his body was on fire. He ditched the hat and gloves and headed out in that misty transition time when the sky turned from a dark gray to a milky white, at the brink of dawn.

It was the first of November. Bitter cold. A light snow falling around him, coating everything in a fine powder. The trend in the weather held steady. It would appear winter was coming early here on Stoner's Mountain and didn't plan on breaking anytime soon. His breath hung in a cloud around his head every time he exhaled. He puffed harder and harder the faster he trekked across the rough terrain. He forged his way through heavy undergrowth off the trail, forcing his body to the limit. Anything to create a distraction. He stomped all the way to the creek. The temperature *had* to be below freezing. It couldn't stop him from stripping out of his clothes. He grabbed a bar of soap and a tube of shampoo from his shirt pocket. Took a deep breath and stepped into the frigid water. Goosebumps sprang up all over his body, his scream echoing off the mountains as the sun crested the horizon.

Ignoring the instinct to run for shore, back to the cozy warmth of his snug cabin, he took a few more steps and dove, immersing his entire body into the ice-cold depths. He shot up for air, his lungs bursting. The fire inside of him had been snuffed out and his mind had been wiped blank of anything except the basic drive to survive. He washed his hair first, dunked under. Came back up and scrubbed all over his body fast and furiously. Eyes closed tight, breath caught in his chest, it was so damn cold! Stay much longer and he'd be a block of ice.

"Are you completely out of your mind?" The incredulous tone of a much too familiar feminine voice nearly had him jumping out of his skin. He plunged back under before whipping around. Stella stood on shore, bundled up to her eyebrows. *Good girl.* Eyes wide with fear. Stuttering. "Or are you trying to kill yourself?"

Stella's eyes popped open about half an hour before the sun woke up. She sat up in her bed, propped against her pillows, laptop on her knees, trying to re-capture the essence of the characters she originally created for her Christmas novel. She banged her fists on the mattress which was completely unsatisfactory. Her leads kept morphing into a man who could be Jesse's twin and a woman who could be her clone. She slammed her computer shut, threw herself back against the pillows, and groaned. *You have got to get it together, Stella. NOW!*

Ordering herself to be disciplined didn't help. Not when her heart, head, and pit of her stomach were much too wrapped up in the mountain man a half hour away. Her mind kept reliving her moments in the crevice, his brave rescue, and the terror of his illness. All intentions of writing came to a screeching halt. What if he had a relapse? He couldn't call, wouldn't come looking for her.

Might not be able to come looking for her.

Stella flew out of bed. She glanced outside and noticed the sky just lightening up. She decided meeting the dawn might help her to shake errant thoughts out of her head. She had to get herself back to the characters who were in her story from the beginning instead of the new ones trying to hijack everything. She quickly washed her face, brushed her teeth, and pulled a comb through her hair. She didn't know why because she was sticking a wool hat on her head. She dressed in long johns under her jeans, her warm boots and coat—courtesy of one mountain man Jesse Collins—gloves And a scarf. She stoked the fireplace to keep the cabin cozy for her return. Satisfied she was prepared, the way Jesse would want her to be, she ventured outside.

Her feet followed the path with a will of their own, wending the way toward his place. Just like her fingers pounded out the story that focused on the man with such a powerful pull, like her personal compass. She'd just check in on him, reassure herself he was all right. He'd probably think she was silly…or annoying. Stella didn't care. Until she saw him with her own eyes, she wouldn't be able to get back to her writing.

She knocked on the door, shifting from one foot to the other. No answer kicked her anxiety levels up. Her hand rested on the doorknob, ready to walk in or break in through a window if she had to, when footprints caught the corner of her eye, footprints not yet covered by the snow coming down. She followed them without hesitation. Images of Jesse sprawled unconscious in the snow pushing her into a jog.

She ignored qualms when the footsteps wandered off the trail. She glanced behind her. Her footprints were clear, the snow light. She figured they'd be better than Hansel and Gretel's breadcrumbs when it came to finding her way back. The snow petered off. It should be all right. *Keep telling yourself that, honey. And if Jesse has to come to your rescue again, what will you do then?* She froze in her tracks. *What if he doesn't come for you because he can't?*

The rush of the creek tumbling through the forest and over the rocks, down the mountain, set her feet back into motion. All her fears, and the ability to think at all, were squashed by the magnificent view.

A honed, toned, beautiful man stood before her in all his glory: hair wet, water streaming down his back, completely naked, the creek coming only up to his knees. Heat rushed through her from the pit of her stomach to the roots of her hair. She pressed her gloved hands to her burning cheeks, certain they'd incinerate, that her whole body would go up in smoke. Her breath spilled out as her heart tripped. The temptation to turn around, go back, pretend she'd never been there was nearly irresistible. But she would never be able to un-see the scene in front of her. She remained as still as a statue, clinging to a tree, fighting the weakness in her knees. When her brain finally started working again, she called out the first words that popped into her head. "Are you completely out of your mind, or are you just trying to kill yourself?"

He ducked into the water and spun around, eyes wildly scanning the forest, zeroing in on her. His eyebrows sprang up, color draining from his face, if that was possible. His teeth chattered as he called out, "What are you doing here?"

She crossed her arms. "Checking on you to make sure you're okay. In case you forgot, you were extremely ill a few days ago. I can't fathom why you have chosen to dive into freezing water in the middle of a deep chill. Do you have a death wish?"

His mouth quirked as he inched his way toward shore. "No. I find this…in…invigorating, but I would like to get out n…n…now. Do…do you mind…a little…privacy…pl…pl…please?"

She whipped around and pressed her forehead against the rough bark of the tree, waiting, struggling against the urge to turn around and watch him. She'd had the full rear view. Now she wanted the front. Minutes that seemed like hours ticked by. She couldn't wait anymore. She turned. Into a tall pillar of a man, trembling, pulling her in close. She wrapped her arms around him and winced. "You're shaking."

He chuckled, the low sound rumbling deep down in his chest. "Of course, I'm shaking! That water is flipping cold!" He grinned and tucked her arm under his. "Come on back to the cabin. It should be really warm. I'll put on something hot. I promise." He took a few steps, turned back, and gave her a hug. "Thanks for checking in on me. I really am okay."

They managed to get back to the cabin without mishaps. Peeling quickly out of his outerwear, Jesse tugged on thick woolen socks, stuck a kettle on the woodstove, and filled two mugs with piping hot water, tea bags, honey, cream. He handed one over, sank into a chair with the woodstove door open and hunkered over his mug as he sipped at it. Stella giggled. "Can you get any closer?"

He quirked an eyebrow. "I'd climb in if I could." He clinked cups with her. "To warm places, hot drinks, and good friends."

"To good friends," she echoed. She sat back, watching him carefully as the shivers died down and the color came back to his cheeks. His hair was still damp, curling around his ears. She nodded to herself. He appeared to be all right. He hadn't made himself sick again. *Thank God.*

Jesse tapped her hand gently. "I've been talking to you, but I don't think you heard me. What would you like to do today?"

She should be industriously hammering the keys on her computer in her cabin, making her publishers happy. Her book didn't stand a chance. A day with him trumped anything else. "Go to town?"

Shadows darkened his eyes for a moment, a muscle twitching in his jaw, but then his smile came out, pushing the darkness away. "I'm about due. To town it is."

He had to make a conscious effort to ease his pace as they worked their way down the mountain. Jesse had become a seasoned hiker. His companion was not, yet she didn't complain, keeping up with him even if her breathing was a bit labored. It was a godsend he had the spare boots and warm outerwear, or Stella would have been a block of ice before they made it halfway to town. Her rosy cheeks and sparkling eyes could stop him in his tracks if he looked at them too long. So, he kept his gaze forward, on the lookout for any icy spots or drifts, anything that could cause trouble. The last thing he needed was for her to turn an ankle…or worse. That would mean medical assistance, authorities, questions, and attention he wanted to avoid. He'd managed to live under the radar in the few months since his arrival. He intended to keep it that way.

"You seem so far away. What's on your mind?" Stella's voice was faint. She was breathless, leaning on a tree a few feet behind him.

He circled back and motioned to the boulder beside them. She gratefully sank on to nature's bench to catch her second wind. He leaned against it, arms crossed. "Just studying the trail. There could be hidden pitfalls. I don't want you to get hurt."

She leaned her head against his shoulder. "You would never let me get hurt. It's not in your nature."

I wouldn't be so sure. I couldn't protect my mother. I can't promise I'll be able to protect you. He argued with his inner voice, reminding himself that he was no longer a little child and much more capable than ever before. *Nearly capable of murder.* Frowning, he pushed off the rock and offered her his hand. "We need to push on. Otherwise, we'll be coming back after dark."

She didn't say a word, stood up, and matched him step by step the rest of the way. The girl was made of tougher stuff than he realized. They emerged on to the trailhead, then the road wending its way into town. It was quiet, not a car in sight. An hour later, they turned on Main Street. The sleepy town had little foot traffic, or any kind of traffic for that matter. The air had a bite to it, the clouds threatening. The possibility of another snowstorm was keeping most people indoors. Stella voiced his thoughts, "It's really quiet. Almost like a ghost town."

"Just the way I like it." He tucked her hand in the crook of his arm and escorted her across the road, pulling up short in front of a diner. "Would you like something hot to drink?"

She clapped her hands together, reminding him of a child at Christmas time. "Oh, yes please! My toes are beginning to turn into a block of ice. The rest of me isn't far behind."

He snickered and brought her inside, introducing her to their server, a young woman named Yvette. "We'll take two of your Moose Track specials, please, and…" he scanned the case of pastries. "Two of those delicious eclairs."

Stella's smile bloomed with a sip of her coffee as they searched for a table. "Wow! This is incredible!"

He grinned. "Best kept secret in town. I found out the first day I came here. Someone told me this little hole in the wall had the best coffee and baked goods in the world. One taste and I was hooked." He gestured to a corner booth with a slight bow and sat beside her, enjoying the unaccustomed treat. They were few and far between growing up. He counted on one hand the number of times his mother baked cookies or cupcakes like all the other mother's at school.

Stop thinking about what she didn't do! You know she had no choice.

He took another sip of coffee when the bell clanged over the door, signaling another customer's arrival. "Hey, Yvette!" A cheerful, deep voice rang out. "Can you get me the usual for the chief?" The hair on Jesse's neck stood up, his body going stiff as he caught the dark uniform and shiny badge on the pocket out of the corner of his eye. He hunkered over his pastry and ate faster, the eclair suddenly tasteless. He was eager to get out.

"Sure, Charlie, but don't you think he could use some sugar for a little sweetening up?" The girl behind the counter bantered playfully with her regular.

Jesse welcomed the distraction. He stood up suddenly and motioned to the door. "Ready? We'd best get moving."

Stella didn't argue, taking one last bite, bringing her cup with her. If she noticed his hasty departure, she didn't say anything while he ducked his head to avoid notice and they hurried across the street.

The moment they walked in the store, he received a cheerful greeting. "Mountain Man! It's good to see you! I was worried about you, what with all the snow we've had. Go ahead in back for your phone call." The owner poked a thumb over her shoulder.

"Thank you. Sally, this is my friend Stella, Stella, Sally Ambrose." He turned to Stella. "I'll be out in a few. Go ahead and pick out anything you need. Just remember we don't have a pack mule."

She smiled, tamping down his fears, calming his nerves. She had a way of doing that. He dialed the number stamped on his heart and waited, and waited, tapping his foot, pacing back and forth by the desk, arguing with himself all the while. *It doesn't mean something happened to her! She could be out! She's not a prisoner. She's allowed to go out!*

After twenty rings, he fought the urge to slam the receiver down on the desk. He stepped out and got his supplies, ringing up Stella's as well. She watched him carefully. "What is it? Bad news?"

He shook his head with a jerk. "No news." He waved a hand when Sally tried to give him his change. "Don't worry about it." Jesse pushed toward the door. He had to get outside, the walls closing in. He couldn't breathe. He turned back at the last second. "Could I try one more time?"

The older woman smiled kindly. "Of course, honey. You go ahead. It will give me a chance to get better acquainted with my favorite author." She winked at Stella and set a copy of her latest book in front of her. "Would you please sign this for me? I'm as giddy as a schoolgirl right now!"

Jesse slipped inside the office and closed the door behind him. Images of his father finding his mother and destroying her made him break out into a cold sweat. He dialed the numbers one more time with more force than needed. Again. Nothing. "Dammit!"

He thumped his fist on the desk and walked out, waving in thanks to the busy cashier. Stella hurried to keep up with him as they stepped out. "What's wrong?"

"I can't talk about it." Putting his greatest fear in words would make it real, too real. The thought of his mother dead, lying in a pool of blood, his father standing over her with a maniacal grin made Jesse stagger. He pressed his back against the building, his legs too wobbly to hold him. Hands on his knees, bent over, sucking in air like a fish out of water. His vision went fuzzy, dots swimming in front of his eyes. Stella's hand rubbed his back reassuringly, giving him the only tether that kept him from completely losing it.

"I think you need to talk to someone." Her voice was almost too quiet to hear.

He snapped up, drawing himself to his full height and glared at her. "You mean therapy?" His voice shook, his entire body quivering as he let out a bark of laughter. "I had therapy. Court-mandated therapy because I beat my father to keep him from killing my mother. I'd do it all again, jail, anything to keep her safe. No amount of counseling will take away the reality my mother and I lived with every day, growing up with a monster. It won't take away the threat of a man who has one goal in life and that's to hurt the only person who ever mattered to me!" He winced at the fear in her eyes as his voice grew louder and louder in volume. "I couldn't protect my mother when I was a boy, wasn't big enough, strong enough. I am now. I got her away from my father, far away, someplace he doesn't know about. Every two weeks, I come to town to check in on her…to make sure he hasn't found her…*and she didn't answer!*"

Stella took his hands and gave them a hard squeeze. "Look at me. Breathe. Just because she didn't answer doesn't mean something bad happened."

His shoulders hunched as he shrank in on himself, making himself smaller. "But something bad always happened in our house."

The shopkeeper stepped outside. "Mountain Man, you've got a call."

He rushed inside, behind the counter, into the office, grabbing the phone like it was a lifeline. Stella stood by his side, holding on tightly to his shoulder. "You're okay. Thank God. You're okay." He couldn't keep his voice from trembling, listening intently, one tear trickling down his face. "I love you, too." He hung up and scraped one hand across his cheek.

The woman at his side threaded her fingers through his. "Why don't we head back? We've got a good hike to get home."

He didn't argue, murmuring, "Thank you," to the shopkeeper before stepping outside. The bell rang over the door cheerfully. Inside of him worry and fear set in. Fear that he would never be able to leave his past behind.

"Does your mother have someone she trusts to look after her where she is now?" Stella asked breathlessly, working hard to keep up with him as he pushed his way home, anger and anxiety fueling his steps.

He shook his head. "The only someone she has is her friend that lives in the same town and took Mom in until she could get settled. The fewer people who know about my mother's whereabouts, the better. I don't even use her name. I've done everything I can to make sure our monster never gets to her again."

"What if he does?"

"It will be over my dead body."

Or his.

Chapter Nine

The manager of the bookstore politely tapped Stella on her shoulder. "Excuse me, Ms. Blair. You have an important call."

She glanced up at the tall, thin man, his eyebrows knit together in concern. Her heart began to race. Swallowing to wet her suddenly dry mouth, she nodded. Her gaze swept over the line of people waiting for signings. She stood and gave them what she hoped was a convincing smile while inwardly fear shook her to the core. No one interrupted her during any of her writing conferences, meet and greet appearances, or bookstore events. It was her personal policy. The fans had given her the gift of fame. They deserved her undivided attention. "Please pardon me for a moment. I need to accept an urgent call."

She wiped her sweating palms on her pants as the polite man at her side gently took her elbow and led her into his office. He gestured to the cushioned chair behind his desk. "Please make yourself comfortable. All you need to do is press the number one. I'll give you your privacy."

Her legs trembled as she crossed the room, but they managed to hold long enough to carry her to her destination. She leaned on the desk with one hand for support and met his gaze. "Thank you," *What is his name? He deserves to be called by his name!* "Barry. You've been too kind."

He nodded and made a small bow in deference to her. "It's the least I can do for one of my favorite authors and a true lady. Take all the time you need. My office is yours. I'll make sure your guests are comfortable and have refreshments." It was an added touch no other bookstore had offered before.

The door quietly shut behind him. She pressed her palm to her waistband, attempting to settle the storm of nerves that had kicked up, fighting the sense of impending doom pressing down on her. She sank into the chair, took a deep breath, and picked up the receiver. Her finger quivered as she pressed line one. "This is Stella Blair."

"Stell…honey. Your mom had a massive heart attack. You need to come right away. I booked you a flight that's leaving in the next hour. Your driver has already pulled up to the curb. You need to go to Philadelphia International right now. It's flight 202 to Albany." There was a long pause and a shuddering breath on the other end. "Sweetheart, I'm so sorry." Her best friend's voice shook, and the line disconnected.

Stella rested her head on the oak desk, gripping the edge until her knuckles went white. Angie Jackson, tough as nails and scrappy as hell, had been her thick-and-thin sidekick since kindergarten. Her friend joined her at college, became an agent, and pushed her first novel in front of every publisher. Angie banged down doors, camped out if she had to, catapulting Stella Blair to stardom. The girl never cracked. If she was on the verge of breaking now, it was bad—

—really bad.

Stella stood up, swaying for an instant. *Grow a spine, girl. Mama needs you.* The tough voice inside, much stronger than how she felt, propelled her out of the room where the manager took her hand. "Your agent has already filled me in. I've informed your fans. Allow me to show you to our side entrance."

She raised her hand in the air. "No, please. I need to say goodbye." She swept a hand under her eyes, wiping away tears, a pointless gesture. They kept streaming down like a tap that couldn't be turned off as she stepped out to meet the crowd. A sea of concerned faces waited for her. So giving and supportive. Her readers were the best, like true friends bonded by the worlds she created in words. "I'm so sorry, everyone, but I must go see my mother. She's suffered a heart attack and I'm afraid the situation is dire. Please leave your name and address with Barry. I will make sure you all get signed copies sent to you free of charge. Forgive me for wasting your time."

An older woman broke away from the crowd to take her hands, so much like her mother, it sent a chill up Stella's back. "My dear girl, it's your mother, just like your novel, 'My Mother's Heart.' We understand. Go to her." Impulsively, she gathered the author in for a hug. Stella held on, inhaling deeply, a fist squeezing around her heart. The stranger even smelled like her mother. The woman patted her back. "There, there, honey. There, there."

A gentle hand squeezed her shoulder. "Miss Blair, I must take you to the airport now or you will miss your flight."

Stella turned to the broad-shouldered, gray-haired man in a suit and cap. The driver resembled her grandfather, one of her favorite people. Reminding her, as with all the other strangers that had helped her that day, angels always found her when she needed them most. *That should be your next book.* Her fists clenched at her sides. *How can you think about books at a time like this?*

She nodded to the driver, thanked the manager, and waved to the fans. Going through the motions as she sat in the back of the car, gripping her purse, numb. Closing her eyes, scenes from her life, featuring her mother, played out in her mind. Just like the scenes in her books, they'd always been comforting to her and a refuge anytime she felt lost and afraid, like now.

The flight was a blur with no chance of sleeping even though she was exhausted. As soon as the plane touched down, a flight attendant hurried to her seat. "Ms. Blair, let me escort you to the exit. A driver is waiting for you at the entrance to the airport."

Finding words, something she did for a living, was a struggle. The attendant, with kind eyes and a gentle touch, took her hand and led the way. Stella turned to the small woman—she had to be at least a foot shorter than her—with midnight hair tucked in a bun, sweet chocolate eyes, and almond skin. *She'd make a wonderful character.* Stella stamped out the thought about writing, wondering what on earth was wrong with her to be thinking about such things at a time like this. She hugged the stranger quickly. Because in times of trouble, when strangers came through with the gift of kindness, they deserved to be recognized. "Thank you. Thank you so much."

She hurried off the plane, cursing her impractical heels for slowing her down; Stella ended up taking them off and running in her stockings. A chauffeur stood in the waiting area holding a sign with her name on it. The fact that he'd managed to get past security to find her, not to mention his anxious expression, only made her quake even harder inside. He caught her eye and waved, "Ms. Blair, right this way. The car is parked out front."

"Thank you." She didn't dare ask for an update, couldn't bear to hear it now. He didn't volunteer. They appeared to be on the same wavelength. Some news was better left unsaid as long as possible. "Please hurry."

"I'll do the best I can, miss." His expression was grim as he glanced in his rearview mirror and pulled out into the flow of traffic. The fates were kind, clearing a path for the fifteen-minute drive to the hospital. He pulled up to the entrance, jumped out, and opened her door. "I'll be waiting for you whenever you need to go anywhere else, Ms. Blair. I'll be praying for your mother and you."

She thanked him and rushed inside, shoes in one hand, her carry-on left behind in the car with her purse. She only hoped identification wouldn't be necessary. She should have known better when the nurse at the counter lit up, eyes wide, rising to her feet immediately. "Oh my! Ms. Blair! I've read all your books. You must be here about your mother. Right this way."

The young woman, a willowy blond with eyes as green as the swirls in a marble, scurried around the desk and opened the doors to the inner workings of the emergency room. She was fast, darting through the hallway, dodging other medical professionals and equipment. Stella had to jog to keep up, breathless. Finally, she said the words that had been clinging to her tongue since the limo driver picked her up. *Francis. His name is Francis.* For some reason, that was important right now. "Excuse me, miss. Could you slow down a moment please? Can you tell me how my mother is?"

The nurse, probably about four years younger than Stella and fresh out of nursing school, turned and took both her hands. "Your mother's doctor will fill you in. They're doing everything they can for her." She led Stella to a small waiting area with comfortable chairs. "There you go, sweetheart. Dr. Myers will be with you as soon as possible. My name is Vicky. If you need anything, please let me know. Would you like coffee or tea, something to eat?"

"No, no thank you." Stella sat still, shoes still in her hand, waiting for her pulse to slow down. A tall man in a white coat, his salt and pepper hair falling into piercing grey eyes, approached her. His eyebrows formed a v, his gaze locking on to her. At any other time, he would have been an inspiration for a character, but right now his face told a story she didn't want to read. She wanted to run, hide, find out this was all a dream. Instead, she sat, her spine rigid, clinging to her shoes, frozen.

"Stella?" His voice was deep and gentle. He sat beside her and took her hand. "I'm Joe Myers, your mother's doctor and a cardiac specialist here at Mercy." His other hand rested on top of hers, cradling it. "I'm so sorry but your mother is gone." He proved to be worthy of playing the hero in a novel when he said no more, just caught her when she fell into his arms and fell to pieces.

She woke up shaking, tears running down her face. The image of Jesse's face, the pain and the uncertainty pushed back the tide of her memories. The knot in her stomach tightened when she thought of the moment they arrived at her porch. As soon as he dropped off her supplies, she turned to him and gave him a brief hug before stepping back. "Thank you, but I think you should go. I'm…I'm really tired."

It was as if a figurative door slammed in her face as his mouth twisted. He nodded with a jerk, turned on one heel, and left, his footsteps fading into the distance. Stella wondered if she'd ever see him again.

Jesse's chest hurt like he'd been stabbed; his heart had been shredded to pieces. *What did you expect? Telling her you were a convict, and you nearly killed your own father. Oh yeah, the girls will be lining up for a prize like you.*

The voice in his head sounded exactly like his old man.

Did you really think coming here would get you away from him? This is just a change of geography. He's in your head. Jesse veered away from his empty cabin, where the walls would close in on him and smother him, reminding him he was alone—totally alone—and probably would be for the rest of his life. *Except for the monster in your head.*

He trekked through the woods, pushing hard, moving as fast as he could. Slipping. Sliding. Falling down. Lying in the snow, huffing and puffing before growling to fight his way back to his feet. He made for the peak, turned back, and forged his own path off the trail. He didn't want to be any place where other people had been. It was time to get lost for a little while, perhaps lose himself and never find his way back.

The forest grew thicker and darker, the trees pressing in against him. He had to fight for every step. The snow deepened. His feet sank until it reached all the way to his knees. Dampness soaked through his boots, seeped through his socks, and settled into his toes until they ached. His jaw snapped together tightly as he grit his teeth. Hard to believe how painful the cold could get. He'd only experienced such pain once before. One Christmas morning, when he was seven and his father tossed him into the snow in his pajamas without any shoes or socks. For an hour.

He almost lost a few toes.

He flung himself against a tree, hands clenching the bark, fingernails digging in. A scream rose from his throat, from somewhere deep in his soul. Wolves howling at the moon couldn't rival him. Completely spent and frozen to the core, he retraced his steps—

—back to the beaten path.

What have you done? Stella got out of bed and went straight to the shower, letting the hot water pound on her head, hoping it would beat some sense into her, clear out the confusion in her brain. Her inner voice argued. *You barely know him. He could be an ax murderer.* She shook her head at the last thought, even stomped her foot, water splashing everywhere. *You have spent enough time with him to know he's a good person. He saved your life—more than once! You pushed him away because he saved his mother regardless of what it cost him. Sometimes, desperate measures are the only option to conquer evil!*

Stella stepped out of the shower and wrapped herself in a thick robe. She padded through the cabin in her warm slippers, built up the fireplace, and set the kettle on to brew. Pacing took over next as her mind replayed the exchange with Jesse again and again. Anxiety took over next. What if something happened to him on the way home?

It would be her fault.

She should be writing, but her only thoughts now were of her …what did the shopkeeper call him? Mountain Man. The tea kettle whistled, steam drifting through the room. She ignored it. Ran to her bedroom, scrambling to find her clothes, tug them on, and get to him as fast as she could.

Footsteps thumped heavily on her porch. Hysterical laughter filled her head with the words *Fee Fi Fo Fum.* She expected a giant to appear. The door burst open, wind and snow swirling around Jesse as he filled the doorway. His hair whipped around his head. He wore no hat, no gloves, and his jacket was wide open. He gasped for breath, both hands braced on the door jamb. "Stella…" His eyes gleamed, bright with unshed tears, as he sucked in a deep breath. "I couldn't go home without talking to you, explaining myself, making you see. I have *never* hurt anyone except my father, and I had no other choice. He would have killed my mother. You have to believe me! I would never hurt you. Please don't give up on me!"

"I won't. *I can't*." She ran across the room and flung herself at him, her arms winding around his back, pressing her body against him. "I'm so sorry I made you go!"

He buried his head in the crook of her neck. "Please don't shut me out again. Now that you've come into my life…I don't think I could live without you." His body wrapped around her tight enough to become entwined. His head bowed to hers, his cold lips touching down on her mouth. Her fingers threaded through his hair, and she melted into him, the heat rising between them, banishing the chill. His arm swept under her legs, carrying her across the room to her sofa where he laid her down, still kissing her—

—close enough for two to become one.

They stretched out on a blanket on the floor for the rest of the night, drinking tea with plenty of lemon and honey, eating hot soup, touching—always touching. She lent him her warmth; he lent her his strength, soothing each other, drifting off in each other's arms.

Sometime in the middle of the night, Stella woke up. She rolled over on her side. He was asleep—sound asleep—giving her a chance to stare at him to her heart's content. In sleep, he looked vulnerable, younger. Her heart ached thinking about the little boy he used to be: small, lonely, afraid.

His eyes snapped open, meeting her gaze. Her hand hovered over his head, touched down lightly, fingers threading through his hair. A cry climbed up her throat, but she swallowed it. She whispered, "I knew you were a good man from the start. This doesn't change anything. You protected the most important person in your life when she couldn't."

He pulled her close and pressed her head to his chest. "If you'll let me, I'll protect you, too."

The steady thumping of his heart lulled her back to sleep in the shelter of his arms.

Stella's nose tickled. She saw a blend of yellow, burnt orange, and red. Her own personal sunrise painted on the inside of her eyelids, telling her morning had arrived. She opened her eyes, blinked quickly, and turned over to avoid the blast of sunlight streaming through the window. Judging by how bright it was, it had to be well past dawn. She pulled up the heavy blanket Jesse must have wrapped around her and snuggled in. A shuffling across the room pulled her attention toward the door.

Jesse was tugging on his boots, lacing them tightly with jerky movements. Something made him stand up and swing around to face her. He cleared his throat, but his voice was still rough like he'd swallowed sand or been awake much longer than he should have been. He smiled but it didn't push away the shadows in his eyes. "Coffee is ready, but I have to go…. have to go home." He crossed the room and leaned down to kiss her forehead. He turned away.

She reached up and snagged his hand, pulling him back. "You asked me not to shut you out but here you are, slamming the door. *What are you so afraid of?*"

He whipped around to face her, his face twisted. "I'm afraid I'll hurt you." He pulled away and pressed his forehead against the wall. "I'm afraid I'm a monster, just like *him!*"

Stella stood up, shedding a pile of blankets, and went to him. She wrapped her arms around his waist and leaned her forehead on his solid shoulder. "You could never hurt me. You don't have it in you. I think *you're* afraid of being hurt again."

A tremor ran through him, hard enough to make her tremble, and the sobs slipped out in between great, heaving breaths. The dam inside of him finally broke, setting free all his carefully contained emotions. Stella led him back to the rug in front of the fireplace, making a nest of blankets and pillows. She turned on the radio, found something soft and slow, a balm for a ragged soul. She made simple things to eat. Peanut butter and jelly crackers. Soup. Hot chocolate. Darkness fell and they hadn't budged. They snuggled close together and gazed at the flames, the warmth and a human touch working their magic. Jesse gently stroked her hair, speaking so quietly she barely heard him over the crackling of the fireplace. "I…I'm scared."

"Why?" She moved closer, holding on tight, trying to ease the pain in his voice.

"Because I love you, and anyone I've loved has been hurt." He stared at her, the corners of his mouth turning down.

She pressed her palms to his cheeks and leaned in until their noses touched. "Not anymore."

Chapter Ten

Stella's proximity, the heat of her breath brushing against Jesse's skin, her touch shattered him. His head spun, tremors running through him, his knees shaking. She pressed him against the mantel. The warm stone was hot, but this woman? She could melt him down or make him evaporate. She pressed her lips to his, ran her fingers over his chin, jaw, and cheekbones. "I have to tell you…I really like your face. I couldn't see it before."

"With you, I'm brave enough to stop hiding." He closed his eyes, losing himself in the moment; let himself be here, now, not waiting for tomorrow to help him to escape from his monster's clutches, his house, jail, his life—

—savoring the present.

She kissed him again, let it spin out. Her hands wandered to his hair. She pulled back, panting for air, holding a long strand. "You trimmed everything else. Why not this?"

His body went tight. "I…I cut my hair once. When I was a kid. My father roared at me, loud enough for the whole neighborhood to hear him, though no one ever stepped in. No one ever tried to help. They all turned their heads the other way or stared at the ground any time they saw my mother and me, saw the bruises, the fat lips, the cuts. The day I cut my hair, he hit me in the face hard enough to swell my eyelids shut and gave me a mean black eye." He breathed in, pushed the air out, faster and faster, on the brink of hyperventilating. "Then he tied me to a kitchen chair and buzzed off all my hair, screaming at me the entire time." He closed his eyes. "I can *still* hear the screaming in my head any time I get a haircut."

Tears filled Stella's eyes. She stood up on tiptoe and kissed him one more time before wrapping her arms around his neck. Her heart fluttered rapidly against his chest. "Let me give it a try. If it's too much, I promise I'll stop." He swallowed, trying to wet his cotton-mouth, and nodded.

She led him to the table by the window in her sunny, bright kitchen. He lowered himself in a chair and stared at her bird feeder, at a female cardinal pecking away. His breath caught as her mate landed beside her, his brilliant red feathers outshining her subdued beauty. "I've always loved cardinals. They're such cheerful birds. When I was little, I'd throw breadcrumbs outside and watch them for hours. Sometimes, I'd pretend I was one of them and we'd fly away together, far away, to a fairytale forest."

Stella gave him a sad smile, one hand resting lightly on his shoulder. "Me too. My mother always said it meant a loved one who passed away was stopping by for a visit." She looked up at the pair and whispered, "Love you too, Mom and Dad."

He reached up, put his hand over hers. "I'm so sorry about your parents. You must miss them terribly."

"I do." She took a shuddering breath but managed to smile even though her eyes gleamed, a sheen of tears close to the surface. "But I'm so grateful to be blessed with them for as long as I had them in my lives. I was only five when Dad died. He was a fireman. He gave his life doing what he loved. He saved an entire family, even their pets. Mom did her best to be both parents." Stella jutted her chin toward a picture she'd propped on the windowsill below the feeder. "She was larger than life with such a big heart. I guess it just couldn't keep beating after loving me so hard. My mother gave me everything she had in her."

Jesse skimmed his thumb over the photo, her warm eyes, gentle smile, and soft curls. He marveled at the way she tilted her head. "She's you in a few years."

Stella laughed. "That's what people always told us. I get my looks from her. My imagination and adventurous spirit are gifts from my father." She walked away, leaving the scent of her perfume or her shampoo lingering by him as if she still stood before him. A moment later something old-time drifted through the room from the radio in the living room. The refrigerator door swished open and clicked shut, the water tap turned off and on. Seconds later, she returned to his side. She draped a towel over his shoulders and handed him a beer. "Drink some of that first." She winked and dipped a comb in a glass of water. Her quiet humming along with the radio set him at ease while her hips swayed back and forth. The comb gently swept through his hair, dampening the strands, hypnotizing him.

He could stay here, in this room, in this chair, with her.

Forever.

He finished the beer, closed his eyes, and relaxed. On the verge of sleep, the first snip of the scissors had him sitting bolt upright in the chair, heart pounding, like an electric shock coursed through his veins. His eyes flew open. "I...can't. I don't think I can..."

She set the comb down, moved between his legs, one hand running through his hair, dipped in, and kissed him, murmuring, "Of course you can. Put your hands right here." She set them on her hips. "Close your eyes again. Let the music have you."

Her hands continued to stroke his hair, soothing him. This time, he didn't wince when the quiet swish of the scissors whispered in his ear. His hands tightened on her hips, fingertips pressing hard. She didn't pause, simply dropped kisses on the curve of his jaw, his forehead, his cheeks, his ears. Her breath was warm, and she smelled good, like coffee, chocolate, and cinnamon buns all rolled in together. He moaned softly. "Feels…so…good." A shiver ran through him, goosebumps popping up on his skin.

She laughed. "Are you cold?" She bit her lip. "Frightened? Do you want me to stop?"

He shook his head. "No. Please don't. This is the best haircut I've ever had." She kept going until the scissors rattled on the table. Jesse came out of the chair in one fluid motion, taking her with him, one arm hooking her under her knees, the other wrapping around her waist. He carried her to the rug in front of the fireplace, went down on his knees, laid her down, and stretched out beside her. Their legs tangled. Their hands finding their way, learning the roadmap of each other's bodies. He rolled to his back and brought her with him until she was on his chest. Their mouths met again and the heat inside of him was hotter than a furnace.

Her breath came in gasps. "Do you…do you want to go to bed?"

He sat up, took both her hands, and stared at her with complete focus. "Is that what you want?" Because God help him, he would get up and go home if she said no. He would respect her wishes, even if it meant imploding.

Her head dipped. His finger trembled slightly as he pressed it beneath her chin. Her eyes widened. She licked her lips, her golden-brown eyes locking with his as a strand of her honey hair dangled in his face. He squeezed his eyes shut, every muscle in his body going tight. The woman had no idea what power she had over him. She kissed him again and hummed in his ear. "It's what I want. I couldn't stand it if you left right now."

He stood and took her hand, walking with her to her room. He peeled off his clothes first and slipped under the heavy comforter. She did the same and eased her way in beside him. He turned to face her and stroked her hair. He found the strength to let the words slip off his tongue. "We can just sleep."

A slow smile bloomed on her face, making it hard for him to breathe. "I don't want to just sleep." As he shifted, sliding in closer, she whispered, "I need to tell you something. This is my first time."

"Mine too." His eyes burned with unshed tears, but he could hear them in his voice. "I was afraid to give myself to anyone, afraid I might be just like my monster."

She took hold of his face and spoke firmly. "You could never be your monster. You are kind and generous and sensitive. Your mother must be an amazing woman to have raised a man like you despite everything that happened in your home."

Her words healed a raw spot deep inside of him, all the knots in his body unraveling at once. "You don't know how much that means to me to hear you say that." He nestled her in the crook of his arm while she rested her palm on his heart. "How come you never slept with anyone before?"

"I was waiting for the man I wanted to spend my life with before I took a chance." His heart picked up the pace. He rested his hand on hers and waited, holding his breath. "I found him. Right here. Right now."

A slow dance of discovery began, like they had all the time in the world to figure out the next step.

Jesse rolled on to his stomach and propped his chin on his arms, his eyes following Stella's every move, from the shower to the bedroom with a towel wrapped around her head like a genie, to the closet as she stared at her wardrobe. She contemplated an outfit, and her robe dropped to the floor. "That one. I think *that* outfit is perfect."

She turned, a rush of color surging to her cheeks, her eyes sparkling. She shook her finger at him. "Behave. We've been lying around for *three* days! I've got to give myself a kick in the pants and get writing. *Putting on* pants is a good place to start."

She started flicking through her hangers only to gasp as his body made a wall for her to lean on, his lips touching down on the skin just behind her ear, his hands roaming. "I think you should come back to bed…to get some sleep. We haven't had hardly any sleep."

She turned around to hook her arms over his neck and kissed him, hard, before stepping back and speaking firmly. "That will have to tide you over for now." Her face grew serious. "If I don't get this done, I'm going to lose my contract and probably my publisher. I don't want to start searching again. I love my publisher."

He cupped her cheek for only a moment, giving her a smile. "Whatever it takes to keep you happy, that's what I'll do. Why don't you go out to your cozy nook on the back porch? I'll build up the fireplace, make some coffee, something to eat. I'll keep out of your hair. Promise."

"Thank you for being so understanding." She pulled on jeans and a heavy sweater, grabbed her laptop off the dresser, and left the room.

Jesse took his time getting himself together. Something he'd never had the luxury of doing. In prison, they were told when to get up, when to eat, when to go to bed. In his childhood home, his schedule was dictated by his father's presence and mood. But here, Jesse could relax—

truly relax—without any threat to his peace of mind. He showered and put on his clothes…the only clothes he had with him. He really would have to go home, even if it was only to get some more clothes. Once he was all cleaned up, he made the bed with precision corners, another lesson pounded into his head by his father—literally.

He pushed dark memories aside. No room for them here in this sunny place with a soft place to land if he fell and a warm woman waiting for him. He made coffee and oatmeal, the kind from scratch with brown sugar and maple syrup and brought everything on a tray to the porch and froze, just looking at her.

Her fingers were idle on her computer keys, her feet tucked beneath her on the large wicker chair with a thick cushion. Her head was turned sideways as she gazed outside at the bird feeder. Two cardinals, a male and a female, flitted round and round. Perhaps the same cardinals from before. Her eyes glowed in the sunlight, her mouth curved in a small smile, like she kept a secret inside of her, her head tipped to the side. She was completely still, more beautiful than any statue the most talented sculptor could ever make.

He cleared his throat. "Breakfast is served." His voice cracked. Silently, he cursed at himself. *Way to go. Trying to be casual and not cutting it. At all.*

She turned up the power of her smile to full blast and set her computer on the small table beside her. She motioned to the other wicker chair. "Join me. Please."

He handed her a bowl and cup before sitting down with his own, eating slowly, waiting for her response, and getting nervous the longer it took for her to say anything. Making meals for his family had been a nightmare. He never knew what to expect when his father was home. He took a few bites, thought the hot cereal passed muster, and finished it off quickly. Jesse didn't realize how hungry he was. When *was* the last time they ate?

"Mmm. This is really good. Just like Mama's. I bet your mother and mine would have been best friends." She took a sip of coffee. "This is incredible, too. I might have to keep you around. Full time."

He didn't dare to believe anything concerning his happiness could actually happen. Didn't dare to hope. He simply answered, "I'm here for you any time." He finished and glanced at her computer and the blank screen. "How's the story coming?"

Her mouth twisted into a pout that made her absolutely adorable, and just when he didn't think she could get any cuter. "Slow. Slower than a turtle or molasses dripping off a spoon! What am I going to do?" She visibly brightened. "Why don't we go back to bed? Maybe that will help."

"As much as I don't want to say this, I think I ought to go home for a while so I'm not such a distraction. You can come and get me when you've made some progress." He stood and collected all the dishes before bending over her to graze her forehead with a kiss. "Or I'll come back in a day. Maybe a time limit will help fire up those fingers."

He set the dishes in the sink and walked to the door, pulling on his boots slowly. Every fiber of his body begged him to stay put, and so did hers. "Don't go. Please don't go." The tremble in her voice did him in. The touch of her hands on his shoulders finished the job as she turned him around and burrowed against him. "I'll work. I promise. I just don't want to be alone, and I don't want you to sit there in that cabin alone either."

"Are you sure?" He whispered into her hair, twirling one of her curls around his finger. "Maybe I'm supposed to be alone. Look at where I came from, my father, what I did to him." He sank down to his knees and buried his face in his hands. "Maybe it's too scary…being with me."

She dropped down next to him and gripped his arms, pulling them down until their hands were clasped together. "Life is scary. Putting yourself out there and opening your heart to someone else? Terrifying. But you can't stay holed up in your own little corner of the world all by yourself for the rest of your life. I won't let you! You may be afraid to take a chance at having happiness, a new beginning. I don't care what you say. I'm not afraid to take a chance on you."

He pulled her on to his lap and wrapped his arms around her. "I don't know what I did to deserve you. Somehow, I found an angel out here in the wilderness."

She held on tightly as they slowly rocked back and forth. "I think my mother sent *you* to me, my angel without wings, to take away my pain and loneliness. I was so lost when she died, but with you, I can find my way back to myself."

Thanksgiving. For the first time in Jesse's life, he looked forward to the holiday, his heart brimming with gratitude. His mother was safe. His monster was gone with no way to find his son or his wife. Against all odds, Jesse had a beautiful woman in his home, his heart, his bed. Or *her* bed, depending on where they stayed. They took turns. He only set one condition on their relationship. If they were going to make it work, he couldn't hold her back. Any time they were together, they couldn't do anything—dance, talk, hike, enjoy the bedroom—until she finished a chapter. In his mind, it justified spending time with her. The more they were together, the farther her writing moved along. And best of all, any time she sat with her laptop, lost in thought, he could get lost in her as he stared at her to his heart's content.

The day started crisp; the sun was so bright his eyes watered. He ventured outside first thing, before she showed any signs of waking. He chopped wood for a good half hour, working up a sweat, breathing hard, plenty warm enough from his exertions. He stacked it on her porch, more inside on the rack by her fireplace, and built up the fire until the flames licked at the opening to the chimney. By the time she wandered out, hair mussed, rubbing her eyes and yawning, two steaming cups of coffee waited on the table along with a full breakfast of bacon, eggs, and toast. He pulled out a chair for her, leaned over her shoulder, and kissed her cheek. "Happy first Thanksgiving."

She set her palm on his face, turning him her way, landing a long kiss on the lips. "Happy Thanksgiving to you. Why do you say first? First together?"

He sat down across from her. "My first real Thanksgiving. If it happened at all at our house, it was always a nightmare. Holidays were *not* something to look forward to for my mother and me."

"They have always been special for me and my family." She raised her coffee cup. "To holidays of every kind and especially Thanksgiving." Their mugs clinked together, filling Jesse with a contentment he'd never known. Once their plates were clean, they stood side by side at the sink, washing them. Jesse helped Stella to prep the turkey, a monster of a bird, and set it in the oven. She clapped her hands together. "All we need to do now is wait."

Jesse set up a nest of blankets and pillows on the floor, one of their favorite places to be where they could toast by an open fire. He wrapped his arms around her and leaned back. He didn't ever want to let go. His eyelids started to droop as he sat by the fireplace. He tried not to mumble. "Anything you want to do today?"

She propped her head on his shoulder. "I'd love to sit here all day, but I think we should get some fresh air. We have to work up an appetite for a bird this big."

Jesse didn't care what they did. Sit inside. Lie in bed. Walk to California and back. He helped her to get on her gear and put on his. They took a long walk, hand in hand, filling their lungs. He was sure they were breathing in fresh opportunities, breathing out bad memories. Hope flickered inside of him. The more she squeezed his hand, smiled at him, set her mouth on his, the higher the flames grew inside of him. Warming him from the inside and out. Reluctantly, he asked, "Is it time to go back?"

"Yes. We need to make the fixings. Thanksgiving isn't Thanksgiving without sides." She hooked an arm around his waist, and they started the trek back. A light snow drifted down, dusting their hair, eyelashes, and faces. Stella poked out her tongue to catch one first. She laughed at his expression. "It's good! We even used to make our own slushies out of them." She froze. "You've never caught a snowflake?"

Before he could let sadness spoil the moment, he made a silly face and stuck out his tongue. His fist pumped the air. "I caught a mouthful!"

They finished their journey back to her cabin to get her roasted turkey before going to his place. She insisted. He would have a true Thanksgiving in a home of his own. Anticipation built inside of him. Looking forward to today was something new; he used to dread any of the special occasions all the other kids at school went on about. Each one was stressful to him before. Not now, not when she was by his side, working with him in unison like they'd done this for a lifetime. Opening his eyes to what his life could be.

What his life *should* be.

They made the trek to Jesse's place, the roasting pan strapped to an old sled with runners. All Stella had to do was set it on his woodstove to keep it warm as soon as they made it inside.

They stomped snow off their boots, shaking flakes from their hair, laughing. Jesse couldn't resist wrapping his arms around her and tucking her in close. She tilted her head to gaze up at him. He wanted to hold on to this moment, stamp it permanently on his memory. The way her eyes sparkled. How damp strands of hair stuck to her face. The roses in her cheeks. Her smile that made the grief and anger inside of him melt away, filling him with a joy he'd never known before.

She planted a quick kiss on his lips. "I wish I could stand here forever but we've got a feast to prepare!" She put dough wrapped in foil in the coals. Poured wine. Both sipped at it until they were giggling. He was dizzy. She stood, held out her hand as the radio played softly in the background. "Dance with me."

A new song hummed inside of him, thrumming in his veins with every beat of his heart as they swayed round and round, her chin nestling in against his collarbone, his head resting on top of hers. Joy, simple and sweet, rushed through him. *This.* This is what he'd been waiting for his whole life. He never thought it was possible. The music continued to play. The fire flickered in the open door of the woodstove. His feet kept swaying side to side. He never wanted to stop.

Stella covered the table with a pretty tablecloth stashed in the closet. Jesse sliced potatoes while she made stuffing. Sweet potatoes went in the oven with green bean casserole. He raised his eyebrows at that. She waved off his concern. "It's good. Trust me. Couldn't have Thanksgiving without it."

He opened a tube of biscuits and laid them out on a baking tray. They'd be ready but first, he lifted the turkey out of the oven. Stella set his biscuits inside and closed the door. Her cheeks were rosy and sweat was beading up on her forehead. He bent down to kiss her. "Couldn't resist."

She kissed him in return, long enough they both had to lean on each other and take a deep breath. "All right. It will be ready in ten minutes. Let me whip the potatoes."

While she finished, he refilled their wine glasses, set out all the dishes on potholders, and sliced the turkey. He vaguely remembered his grandfather doing it, long ago, one time when he and his mother came by themselves and had a fairytale dinner. That was the time his mother got away from his father and didn't plan on going back. Until his father begged her, cried even, said he had changed his ways. They went back to what they'd always known—torture. Jesse shook his head as if shooing away a fly. He loaded up two plates with Stella's help, and they sat together. She lit a candle in the middle of the table, reached across, and held his hand. "I'm so grateful…so grateful fate or Mom or God and His angels brought me here, to you."

His eyes filled. "I'm grateful. For Thanksgiving. A new life. To learn what love is all about and have you for my teacher."

They ate until they were stuffed and couldn't move. They sat on the porch watching the moon and the stars, wrapped up in a blanket, together. Jesse's arm around her. Stella's head on his shoulder. Snowflakes drifted through the air, swirling slowly in a gentle breeze. She sighed, her eyelids drooping closed, and slipped into a deep sleep. Jesse pressed a kiss to the crown of her head, gazed up at the sky, and whispered, "Thank You. For all of it. For every step that led me here." Sleep took him next, deep enough to be free of dreams or nightmares—

—still tangled in her arms when daylight arrived.

Chapter Eleven

Jesse swung his ax in a great arc and brought it down hard with a satisfying thud. He split a large piece of wood down the middle; each half tumbled into the snow. He picked up another piece and repeated the performance, his smile growing. Working hard felt good while he waited for the next time Stella came to his house. As soon as she finished two chapters, she'd give him two nights.

Eagerness pushed him to move faster. The air whooshed out of his mouth and formed a cloud before he sucked in, filling his lungs. Heat rushed through his arms as the ax came down again. The pile grew almost waist high. Satisfaction made him light-headed. He leaned on his ax for a moment, propped on the stump he used for a chopping block. He closed his eyes, considered peeling off his coat. He was hot from working so hard. It wouldn't surprise him if steam rose off his clothes. *Just need a minute or two and I'll start stacking it.*

"Hoo-ee, *that* is a lot of wood. I'll know who to call if I ever need a lumberjack." A female voice called out cheerfully. A thrill shot through him. *She's early!* Jesse's eyes snapped open and locked on a short, voluptuous stranger in a crimson coat and winter cap as bright as a cardinal. The brilliant splash of color on her lips matched it perfectly. Her eyes, a rich chocolate, complemented her ebony skin perfectly. She was a thing of beauty and looked completely out of place in high-heeled boots, thin leather gloves, and a beret that while stylish did nothing to keep her head or ears warm. He could see her shaking with a chill from the deep snow she'd trudged through and the uncertainty in her gaze when she stammered, "Right now, I need a guide and I'm really praying you're not an ax murderer because I am hopelessly lost and freezing!"

How many damsels in distress are going to show up at my doorstep?

Remembering his manners, he stepped forward and extended his hand. "I'm Jesse, and I'll do my best. Why don't you come inside to warm up and we'll figure out what direction you need to go. I promise, I'm not an ax murderer."

She must have been desperate enough to trust him, even though he held an ax, because her hand gripped his tight enough to hurt. "Oh, thank you! Thank you! Thank you! I've been walking for what feels like hours. I parked at the trailhead and followed the sign, but then I got off course somehow and these awful boots are soaked through to the skin!" She stumbled along beside him, tugging on a suitcase with wheels that were totally useless in the snow.

"Let me get your case for you." He pushed the handle in and picked it up with his free hand, allowing her to lean on him as they made their way up the steps to his cabin. He closed the door and led her to the recliner by the wood stove. "Sit right here and I'll get you something hot to drink. Coffee, tea, or hot chocolate?"

Ever since Stella started visiting regularly, he'd expanded his repertoire of refreshments. He might not mind roughing it, but she deserved life's simple pleasures. He set a kettle on the woodstove and his percolator. He needed coffee, black, to stay alert, to handle this unexpected visitor in his home. Paranoia reared its ugly head. What if it was a reporter? A detective intent on leading his monster to his doorstep? He busied himself with setting out cups and fixings, balling his hands into fists—

—willing them not to shake.

The woman leaned forward and held her palms up to the woodstove. She'd already stripped off her impractical gloves. She sighed and her eyes closed. "Oh. I never thought heat could feel this good."

He cleared his throat. "You really need to take off those wet boots. You could have the beginnings of frostbite." He walked over to her and knelt on the floor. "Mind if I help?" At a shake of her head, he undid the zipper on one, eased it off gently, peeled off her soaked sock, then moved on to her other foot. "Did you decide what you want to drink?"

"Whiskey?" at his raised eyebrows, she laughed. "Just kidding. Coffee would be fine, heavy on the cream and sugar." She wiggled her toes. "Thank you. Thank you so much. That is much better. I am woefully unprepared for a trek through the wilderness." She extended her hand to him. "I'm Angie, by the way. It's a pleasure to meet you. I can't thank you enough for coming to my rescue."

He waved her off, hanging her socks to dry over the wood rack. He went to his dresser and pulled out a pair of wool socks, fingering them. The same socks he loaned to Stella the day she arrived. Holding them brought back the memories of holding her. The room tilted for a moment. He held on tight to the dresser and found his center. Stella Blair turned his world upside down.

He returned to the woman by the stove. "Put these on to warm up." He lifted the coffee pot off the stove with a potholder and poured two steaming mugs. He kept his black but doctored hers. He carefully set the cup in her hands. "Careful. If you're used to electric coffee pots, this is a lot hotter."

"I'm so cold I feel like I could guzzle the whole pot right now." She took a sip, her mouth curling up in a satisfied smile. "Mmm. That is perfect and so much better than anything from an electric pot—or a coffee shop in the city. You've got something here."

Jesse pulled a chair away from his table and perched on the edge of his seat. Feeling like he was about to fall into a pit of the unknown. He buried his fears, took a long draw on his coffee to fortify himself and make conversation like a normal person—something he'd never been. "So, what brings you to this neck of the woods? Please don't be offended but you look a little out of place."

Her mouth twisted as she took another sip of her coffee. "No offense taken. I'm a city girl, through and through. I've never been camping or on a hike. My idea of exercise is to dash down the sidewalk to hail a cab. I came here to check up on a friend of mine, and now I'm not even sure I'm in the right place. I don't suppose you have bumped into Stella Blair out here in the wilderness?"

He sputtered, choking on his coffee, and raised his hand. "I'm all right. Sorry. Yes, I've met her. She's about a mile farther up the mountain. I'll be glad to lead you there if…" A knock sounded on the door. "If she doesn't get here first."

The door flung open before he even had a chance to stand up. "Holy moly, it's freezing out there." The woman in question burst inside, a blast of wind following her, bringing a dusting of snowflakes with her. She shoved the door closed and leaned against it, eyes squeezed shut, huffing and puffing. "I finished my chapters. I don't know if they're good or not, but they're done so now it's time for you and me…" She broke off as her gaze fixed on the woman hunkered down by his wood stove. "Angie! What are you doing here?"

She raced across the room, heedless of wet boots or the fact that her hat, hair, eyelashes, and coat were covered in snow. Her nose and cheeks were scarlet from the frigid temperature, eyes glittering brightly. The cold looked good on her, as usual. Angie stood up and met her halfway, flinging her arms around her. "Girlfriend, I had to make sure you were okay. You dropped off the face of the earth. You don't know how much work it took to track your tail down. I was going to leave you alone, but then I thought, you aren't any more of a wilderness girl than me. What if you were a frozen block of ice up here? So, I caught a plane, rented a car, and here I am. If it weren't for Mr. Tall, Dark and Ruggedly Handsome over there, I'd be floundering around out there, becoming a snow sculpture."

Stella laughed, only to put her mittened hands to her cheeks. "Oh, Jesse!" She reached out, snagged his hand, and pulled him into an embrace, her lips finding their way to where they belonged. "I'm so sorry! I didn't even give you a proper hello." She kissed him one more time. "How's that?"

He rested his forehead on hers and let go the breath he didn't know had been pent up inside. "Better than anything I ever hoped for." His arms wrapped around her, reeling her in snug against him. All he wanted to do was hold on tight. A knot in his gut gave a hard tug.

Fearful this stranger *would* take her away from him.

Stella leaned into him and whispered huskily, "I can say hello again if you'd like." A quiet cough from the other woman in the room brought the color surging even more brightly to her cheeks. "Oh, Angie. I'm so sorry. He's hard to resist. I see my Mountain Man came to your rescue too. Jesse, Angie is my best friend and agent, who I'm sure is not *only* checking up on my well-being. I *have* been writing. You really didn't need to come all the way out here." A storm brewed in her eyes, her eyebrows and mouth forming a stern line, but she couldn't hold it. She squeezed her friend's hand. "I'm glad you did. I've missed you."

"I missed you, too," Angie sniffled before burying her face in her mug, brushing away a tear from the corner of her eye.

Jesse forced himself to move. Keeping himself busy all his life was the only thing that saved him. "How about a hot drink, and then I'll accompany you back to your cabin? Tea or coffee?"

"I'll have the same as you two. Make it sweet," Stella winked and blew him a kiss.

Jesse really didn't have to ask. He knew she liked tea best in the morning. Coffee in the afternoon. Hot cocoa before bed. No matter what, something hot to warm her up, but he made it his mission to be the best heater around. He quickly made her a cup and propped his elbow on the counter, gaze trained outside, listening to the quiet chatter from the next room, giggles, the give and take between two people who had been in each other's lives forever.

How could he possibly compete?

Stella gave Angie a pair of flannel pajamas, a thick blanket, and a cup of tea once they settled in at her cabin. They quietly sipped the steaming brew while her agent slowly overcame a deep chill, her tremors calming down. Stella gazed out the window, chin propped on her palm, staring at Jesse's retreating footsteps long after he'd faded into the distance. As darkness fell, a shiver ran through her that had nothing to do with the cold. She feared he might not come back.

Her best friend squeezed her knee. "I'd be staring out the window with longing if someone like your Mountain Man was hanging around me. So, tell me about him. Spill it all, like you would about a character in your novels. You know, one of your favorite characters that you fall in love with and make the star of a never-ending series."

Stella set her cup aside and drew her knees up, feet hooked on the edge of her chair. "What you see is what you get. He's kind, strong, filled with courage." A fierce need to shield him surged up inside of her. She had always confided in her childhood friend about *everything*…but Jesse's secrets did not belong to her. "I went to his cabin first the day I arrived on the mountain just like you. And like you, I was not prepared to rough it in the wilderness." She shook her head ruefully. "You don't know how many times I berated myself for not doing my homework…and me, an acclaimed novelist known for her in-depth research for any project."

"And your Mountain Man came to the rescue, just like he did for me." A dreamy look drifted into Angie's eyes. "Honey, he is one fine specimen of a man. Lean, honed. Muscles in all the right places. That chiseled jaw, those brooding eyes that can see right through you, that dark hair falling into his face to form a place to hide when he needs it. I see the way he looks at you."

The heat flared in Stella's chest, creeping upward until her ears and cheeks were hot. "I don't know what you're talking about."

Angie took both of her hands in a firm grip and stared her down. "Now, Stell. You have never lied to me. Don't start now. That man looks at you the same way you look at him. If I had someone like him, I'd be giving up my career to be a hermit, no doubt about it. I don't know how you've managed to write one word with such a powerful distraction tugging on your heart, mind, and soul."

Stella stood up and grabbed her laptop. She opened it up, tapped some keys, and set it in her friend's lap. "I can prove you wrong."

Four hours later, Angie set the computer down long enough to wipe her face with a tissue helpfully placed within reach. She looked up at Stella, nervously perched on the edge of the couch, struggling not to bite her nails since she'd never taken it up before, and gave her a tremulous smile. "Prove me wrong? It's the best work you've ever done. I need to get out of your way."

The sky was unobscured by snowflakes or clouds, a rarity. Moonlight spilled through Jesse's window, turning the woman in his bed into a marble statue. He stared at her intently, holding his breath, afraid Stella had been trapped by a spell. The air hissed slowly between his teeth when her chest rose and fell. He imprinted everything about her on his brain. The way her hair curled around her ear before tumbling over her shoulder to fan out on her pillow. How her mouth tipped up at the corners, even in her sleep. Ever the optimist. The soft melody of her sigh as her body shifted close enough for him to feel her warmth seeping through his pajamas.

He could stay right here, right now, forever.

He turned on his side, leaned on his elbow, and propped his head on his hand, watching, waiting for the dawn to paint her with light. Refusing to let sleep pull him under again, he wanted to see her the moment her eyes opened and lit up to see him. She shifted again. He couldn't resist reaching out to stroke her cheek. "Mmm. Feels good." Her eyes opened, and her smile grew. "Come closer." He didn't argue as her arm wrapped around him, and she pressed his ear to her chest, soothing him with every beat of her heart.

The bed jolted as he jerked awake, his eyelids snapping open to an empty bed. He rolled over and reached for the other pillow. Cold, cruel dream—she'd never been here. *And probably won't be here much longer now that real life has shown up to reel her back in.*

Anger, despair, and a crushing depression rolled over him, strong enough to pin him to his mattress if he let it. He pushed it back, like he had every other bit of unpleasantness in his life and got out of bed. He built up his woodstove, took a shower, shaved, and drank a cup of coffee but avoided breakfast with the way his stomach rolled. He went through the methodical process of dressing warm enough for the elements: thick socks, heavy boots, his warm coat, hat, gloves. He hooked his pack on his back and ventured out. Glancing back, the smoke in the chimney was a small reassurance that something warm would be waiting for him when he returned.

The only thing he could count on.

The trip into town went faster than usual. Jesse didn't realize how hard he'd pushed himself until buildings came into view. He had to prop himself on a tree to catch his breath, then closed the gap to the store. Sally gave him a welcoming smile and waved her hand when he walked in. "Mountain Man! Happy Thanksgiving! It's a blessing to see you here, healthy and strong."

"I could say the same about your cheerful face, Ms. Sally." He went about his business, restocking his basic supplies, paying her, and filling up his pack.

She motioned to her office. "Go ahead and make your call. Take as long as you need." Her hand on his back reminded him of his mother as she gave him a pat, bringing tears to his eyes.

The door closed behind him with a click. He dialed and waited, heart hammering, lungs ready to burst because he couldn't breathe, not until she answered…and then she did. "Happy Thanksgiving. Sorry I couldn't call sooner. How are you?"

"Good. Really good. I'm still stuffed with turkey. I ate with good friends. It was the best Thanksgiving I've ever had. The only thing missing was you." Her voice choked with tears. "I miss you, baby."

"I miss you, too. I'll talk to you soon. Love you." He gripped the phone tightly, holding on long after she whispered, "Love you more," wishing he could hold on to her like he did as a little boy, his small hand tucked into hers.

The safest place in the world.

He mopped the tears from his face and hung up. Took a moment to collect himself and stepped out into the store. He turned to say goodbye to Sally and caught her speaking to someone with a familiar profile. Tall. Patchy gray hair. Shoulders hunched. Gravel in his voice. If the man turned around, Jesse was sure the eyes would be as brown as a puddle after a storm, a web of red lines rubbing through the whites. Jesse ran outside with his hand pressed to his chest, fighting the tight fist squeezing his lungs. He darted around the corner and hunkered down by the side of the building, head bowed trying not to be sick. How…how could his monster be *here*? And if he could be here, how long would it take his father to find his mother?

The need to protect her, no matter the consequences, had to come first. Not the terror coursing through his veins or the overpowering rage that threatened to consume him. He drew himself to his feet and rushed toward the door, a roar rising in his throat only to stop as if his feet had become planted in the ground. The man he'd been watching stepped outside and glanced at him, winking an eye as brilliant as an emerald and giving him a crooked grin. "Good afternoon." His grin faded away as Jesse swayed, his legs about to buckle. "Are you okay? You don't look so good."

Jesse waved him off and turned around, taking one step at a time even as he started to shake uncontrollably. The farther he walked, the steadier he became. Doing his best to put the nightmare behind him where it belonged, he set his sights on the cabin. Walking slowly at first, until a candle lit inside of him, urging him to go home.

And her name is Stella.

"It's time for me to get back where I belong so you can do what you do best." Angie stood at the door, suitcase packed, dressed to brave the elements.

Stella flung her arms around her friend. "But you've only been here two days. Stay a week. We can have some girl time. You can find out what it's like to truly get away from everything for a while. I'll work, pinky promise." She held up her little finger. "I'll invite Jesse over so you can spend more time admiring him."

"Sweetheart don't tempt me. It wouldn't be beneath me to try to steal him away from you if I didn't know it was a lost cause." Angie hugged her hard enough to squeeze the air out of her lungs...and maybe her stuffings too. "I need to go. You've got too much to do and too little time to do it. You can't afford to spend a week on me."

Stella held on even tighter. "Honey, I'd give you a year if you needed it...or longer. Only say the word and I'm yours." She let go, put on her boots, coat, winter hat, and gloves. "Since I know there's no talking you out of something once you've made up your mind, I'm walking down with you."

"I'd argue with you but there's no sense in it. You're too stubborn. Must be why we're best friends." The day was mild, no snow drifting down, making the trek down considerably easier than the trip up the mountain. An hour later, they stopped at Angie's car, parked next to Stella's at the trailhead parking area. Except for their lone vehicles, there wasn't another soul in sight.

"I guess this isn't the time of year for tourists." Stella held on to her best friend's open car door. "I really wish you could stay."

Angie stood up and gave her a hug and kiss on the cheek. "We both know I'm not what you need right now, Stell. Otherwise, I'd have been here since the start. You've got about three weeks, girlfriend. I know you'll be ready. Love you to pieces."

"Love you more." Stella stepped back, allowing her friend to start the car. "Drive carefully!" She waved with all the enthusiasm she could muster; on the inside, her heart was breaking. She kept waving, her glove like a flag flapping in the wind until Angie's taillights faded into the distance. Stella bit her lip, arms wrapped around her waist. *You need to have an ugly, all-out cry about now.* She stood still for a few more minutes, her breath forming a cloud around her, waiting to settle herself, gather the shreds of her composure, and go back. She spun around and walked into a wall of muscle, skin, and bones. She gazed up into Jesse's face, tormented and whiter than the snow beneath her feet.

His hands gripped her arms, his eyes glistening. "I thought you were leaving without saying goodbye. I saw you walking with Angie…and I thought it was over."

She sealed his mouth with a kiss and pulled back to look him in the eye; her gloves pressed to his cheeks. "I couldn't do that to you; I couldn't say goodbye to you. Ever."

He ripped himself away from her and paced, wearing a track deeper and deeper into the snow. "Why *wouldn't* you say goodbye to me? You have a life, a much better life than anything I could offer you. The best thing you can do is go, forget you ever met me. Forget all of this while I hole up all by myself. I'm not fit company for anyone. Angie and the city have to be calling you. You don't need this place to find your creative spark. It was inside you all along." His voice rose in volume until he was shouting at her loud enough to cause an avalanche. "You need to go back where you belong!"

She took two giant steps, placing herself directly in front of him. She lifted her chin with a courage and defiance she didn't feel. Putting steel in her voice so she wouldn't crumble in a heap at his feet. "You're *not* going to scare me away. I know the real you. The man who will defend what he loves no matter what it takes, if it locks him up, turns him into something he wasn't before, even if it takes his last breath. Tell me what happened to make you act like this. Seeing Angie and insecurity could be part of it, but there's something more. *Don't hide yourself away from me!*"

Two crimson streaks blazed in his cheeks, the embers of his anger burning in his eyes. Hot enough to make her want to step back, but she planted her feet, hands on her hips, holding her ground. Custer's last stand flashed in her mind. She bit her lip and hoped it wouldn't come to throwing herself at his feet or holding on to his legs if he tried to walk away. *Have to maintain some semblance of dignity.* He continued to glare, only to deflate as the air hissed between his teeth. "I went into town to check in on my mother…and I thought I saw our monster."

He sank down and pressed his back against the trunk of a tree, driving his forehead into his bent knees. Stella sat beside him and wrapped her arm around him, ignoring the snow seeping through her pants, soaking her. A chill ran straight through her, from her head to her toes. "He's not going to find you here. He doesn't know about this place, doesn't know you're out of jail. You don't even know if he's alive."

"Oh, he's alive. The bastard is too miserable to die. The devil himself would send him back to earth." Jesse clenched his jaw. Humorless laughter slipped out. "And he could find me if he wants to badly enough. He's like a cat with nine hundred lives who always gets out of scrapes, always has some insider who is working behind the scenes. No matter how careful I've been, I will always be looking for him. The guy in the store…once I took a good look, clearly wasn't him."

His head snapped up as his gaze locked with hers. "What if he finds me?"

She pulled him in close, drawing his head to her chest. "He won't. You just have to believe that part of your life has been left behind." She held on until his breathing stopped being ragged. "Now, do you think we could get moving to your place? I'm turning into an ice cube out here!"

He chuckled roughly and grazed her lips with his, lighting a flame that went a long way toward thawing her out. "Yes. Of course. I'm sorry." He stood, drawing her with him, his arm around her. He helped her to navigate dips, deep spots, and drifts. When she faltered, he picked her up and carried her the rest of the way to his cabin. Never complaining. Never slowing.

As solid and steadfast as the pines and mountains rising above them.

Chapter Twelve

Jesse held Stella close all through the night, treating her like something fragile that could break at his touch, running his fingers through her hair and along her entire body so gently, she fell asleep. Every time she awoke, he was there, facing her, watching her. His breath skimmed over her skin as he dropped a kiss on her lips. He held out a finger to lift the cross from her chest and pressed it to his mouth before making the sign of the cross. "My mother…used to take me…to church for the holidays after he hurt us, in the rare times when we were alone. I liked church. It was quiet. Safe. Closed off from the rest of the world. The way I feel now."

"I'll be your church." She tucked herself in under his arm, as close as possible, eyes stinging from the image of a little boy with huge blue eyes blazing in a pale face much too thin. With dark shadows in his gaze, huddled against the side of his mother, trying to disappear. Stella rubbed his chest, letting her hand go still over his heart. Its quiet beating, steady as a drum, sent her off to sleep.

The sound got louder and louder, thundering in her head. She gasped. Opened her eyes. Shut them tightly. *No. It's a dream. A nightmare really. It's not real.* Someone squeezed her hand. "Come on, honey. I won't leave your side. I promise." Stella leaned toward the familiar voice, her best friend, Angie, with her through thick and thin.

Stella took a deep breath, a few more steps forward, and looked down. At the woman who brought her into the world and was now leaving it. She fell to her knees by the casket, arms reaching for her mother. "Oh, Mama. How will I live without you?"

"Hey…hey. It's all right. I'm right here." A deep, gentle voice rolled out in the darkness while a firm hand held on to her, keeping her steady. She opened her eyes to see Jesse inches away. He rubbed his thumb over her cheek. "You were crying in your sleep. What is it, sweetheart?"

She buried her head against his shoulder. "My mother…and her funeral." She choked on the last, the tears flowing once again.

His hand trembled on the crown of her head as he stroked her hair soothingly. "I can't bear the thought of my mother being gone. I can accept that she's across the country with only phone calls to assure me she's there…but to never speak to her again?" He swallowed hard. "It would break my heart." He gently kissed her cheek. "I can't fix it or bring her back, but I'm here for you."

She sniffled. "I know."

They held on to each other until sleep came for her again.

"I've never slept in before in my entire life." Jesse held back a moan as Stella's fingers stroked his hair, sending a delicious warmth through his body. *Best therapy a guy could ever get. Beats counseling any day of the week.* He rolled over and returned the favor. He loved how silky her hair was, shining in the sunlight, tumbling over her shoulders and down her back.

She practically purred, sliding closer. "It's my first time too. I feel incredibly lazy when I'm here with you." She sighed and opened one eye. "Are you hungry?"

The rumble of her stomach told him everything he needed to know. He chuckled—deep down in his belly, something new to him—and dropped a kiss on her lips. "I am, although I hate to leave this cozy nest."

She looped her arms around his neck to bring him in for a kiss that snatched his breath away and gave him a completely different kind of hunger. Reluctantly, he pulled away. Otherwise, they'd starve. She patted the bed. "I'll keep your place warm and waiting for you." Her smile and the roses blooming in her cheeks almost did him in.

A whistle spilled out as happiness bubbled up inside of him. He chose not to question it or doubt it, just embraced it for as long as it could last. Breakfast couldn't be ready fast enough, scrambled eggs, toast, and two cups of coffee. All the while, his pulse raced—

—in anticipation of her.

Walking back in with the food on a tray, he almost dropped it. Stella had rolled over, the blanket sliding down to her waist, revealing her beautiful curves in all the right places. One hand rested on his pillow; the other was folded under hers. The sun kissed her skin—

—everywhere that he wanted to touch her.

"Mm. That smells delicious." She rolled over and sat up, bringing up the blankets to cover herself. Sometime in the night, the t-shirt he'd loaned her for a nightgown had become a puddle of fabric on the floor.

His stomach went taut.

He handed her a steaming mug and set his on the table beside the bed. Settling in next to her, he propped the tray on his knees. "Enjoy."

They ate quietly. Because they didn't need to fill the silence. Being together was enough. When it was all gone, she set her plate on the tray and kissed him on his jaw before slipping out of bed. She pulled on his t-shirt and took the dishes to the kitchen. A moment later, she was back in bed. "What do you want to do today?" She propped her head on his shoulder.

He tilted his head toward her. "This. Nothing else. I couldn't imagine a more perfect day."

She inched her way down, taking him with her until they were tucked into each other like spoons. "Then this is it." She patted his hand as he set it on her waist.

"What about your writing?" He murmured in her hair. It smelled heavenly, like wildflowers in the middle of summer in barefoot weather when he and his mother packed a lunch, sat on the dock at a farmer's pond and fed the ducks, watched the fish, laughed. He shook his head, wondering, did that really happen or was it a dream?

Nothing seemed real before Stella.

"It will keep." Her words were heavy and slow as sleep came for her. She tapped her head lightly. "It's all up here. This—right here, right now—is more important."

He didn't question it, didn't torment himself with doubt. He gave himself to the moment and let sleep take him under, on the best day of his life.

They spent hours talking, giving away little bits of themselves, eating in bed. Sinfully lazy, she said. Eventually, they moved to the living room for a little while to lie in front of the woodstove and pick out shapes in the dancing flames. She spun a story for each one and he was entranced, caught in her web. Only when darkness came did they go back to bed, losing themselves in the lullaby of each other.

A thud yanked Jesse from a sound sleep and kicked his heart into high gear. He fought to slow down his breathing, drew himself closer to Stella, convinced himself everything was right in his world for once. He closed his eyes, inhaled the sweet scent of her hair. His body went loose. If he allowed his imagination to take over, he might be able to weave together the threads of a beautiful dream. One in which he belonged to her, and she belonged to him. Her sigh made him smile and sigh along with her.

A louder thud pulled Jesse from his bed, a current of fear sizzling in his veins. Planted on the balls of his feet, bending his knees slightly, hands raised, poised to fight, he peered into the darkness but couldn't see anything. The moon had slipped behind a cloud, plunging the cabin's interior into thick shadows. An even louder noise sent him creeping out of the bedroom. He picked up a log by the woodstove on his way across the room, running his fingers over the rough bark, hefting it in his hand, flexing his arm,   preparing to swing it like an ax or a hammer if need be. No matter what, he would defend Stella at all costs.

Even if it meant giving up his life.

He moved past the kitchen window and hunkered down, unsure if anyone outside could see him. His breath came in ragged pants as he reached his front door. Something shuffled outside. Jesse's mind raced, wondering if a log would be enough to take on an angry, starving bear. More thumps echoed outside along with a rumble of curse words. *Definitely not a bear*. The heavy scent of alcohol, strong alcohol, like someone had been drenched in it, wafted under his door. A type of alcohol he had smelled all his life and knew very well. It was so strong he could almost taste it.

It nearly made him sick.

Jesse's stomach lurched and his heart thundered in his ears even as he pressed himself against the door. The knob rattled. He tensed, driving his back into the heavy wood, doing his best to be a barrier. The lock held. Relief flooded through him so strong, his knees buckled. He dropped down, piece of wood in hand, eyes closed tight, praying that this was all a dream, his imagination—a nightmare. The back door rattled even louder. He pushed himself off the floor, certain a window would be next.

Jesse slipped back into the bedroom and gently shook Stella's shoulder. Doing his best to appear calm. Inside, an earthquake shook him to the core. "I need you to get under the bed. Now. If you hear anything at all, *anything*, you get out. You grab a blanket, boots from my closet, and you run. Run out the door and down the mountain and get yourself to town. Understand me?"

"What is it?" She whispered even while throwing back the covers and crawling under the bed.

"My monster's here, and if he finishes me off, he might find you next. He's drunk, and when he's drunk, he's meaner than mean, and he does things that don't make sense. He's out of his head. No place here is safe. If anything happens to me, you will need to get away as far as you can." He leaned in and kissed her, holding on to her hands and squeezing them tightly.

Please, God. Let me keep her safe. Don't let him hurt her. Please.

The shattering of glass crashed through the silence. He pressed a finger to her lips and slipped out of the room, turning the lock on the door before he closed it behind him.

"Laura!" Moonlight streamed through the living room as the clouds shifted. His father crawled through the broken window, gashing his hand along the way, dripping blood. Cursing. Bellowing, "*Laura!*"

"She's not here, and I promise you will never see her again." Jesse picked up the log he'd dropped on the floor and raised it. Shoulders set.

Jaw clenched. Ready. So ready. To end this once and for all. End his monster. "How did you find me?"

His father laughed harshly. "I climbed your mother's family tree, used that DNA discovery site with a little help from a friend." He tapped his head. "I'm not as stupid as you think I am. It wasn't hard to dig up information about her dear old grandfather and his little cabin in the woods. I can't believe she kept this place secret all these years. I could have had the high life by selling this place. What did I get instead? An ingrate of a son like you."

"You always hated me, didn't you?" Jesse's voice trembled with barely controlled rage.

His father grinned, but it only made his face more frightening. "I hated you from the moment I found out you were coming. I know you're not mine, bastard." His laughter was an ugly bark. "The day she told me was the first time I hit her."

"You'll never hit her again!" The log clattered on the floor and Jesse's fist flew with a will of its own, connecting with his uninvited, unwelcome intruder's jaw. Driving his father back toward the front door, closer and closer with every blow. He rammed him with both palms flat against his chest. His fingers closed like claws around the lapels of his old man's jacket. He slammed him against the door once. And again, even harder, satisfied to hear his head clunk loudly against the unforgiving wood. While his father was dazed and staggering, he opened the door and shoved him onto the porch. He hit him again, sending him flying down three steps. A puff of snow flew into the air as he landed in several feet of powder. "If it's the last thing I do, I am going to wipe you off the face of this earth, so you never come back to hurt *anyone!*" Jesse launched himself off the porch and pummeled his father,

gasping, reliving that night in his childhood home that sent him to jail all over again—

—seeing red.

Stella grabbed Jesse by the back of his shirt, digging her heels in, trying to hold him back. Even as he dragged her forward with him. "He's not worth it, Jesse! Don't ruin your life for someone lower than pond scum. You don't owe him the time of day!" Her words broke through the haze of his fury, and he froze.

Something in Jesse's eyes must have kept his monster's mouth shut, had his father scrambling backward on all fours, fighting to get to his feet, going white as if he'd seen a ghost. He stammered, "I'm going. Right now. You won't see me again. Ever! I promise! You and your mother don't ever have to worry about me anymore." Jesse took one step toward him, putting all the menace in his heart into his face, drawing himself up to his full height, fearful his head would explode with steam shooting off the top from the heat of his anger. "Dear God, please don't kill me!" His father turned and ran blindly back the way he came just as the skies unleashed a snowstorm of blizzard proportions, wind whipping, temperature dropping, blinding.

Jesse turned around, wrapped an arm around Stella, and brought her inside with him. He slammed the door shut and pressed his back against it. He held on, waiting for the storm raging inside of him to die, for his racing heart to slow, to breathe again. She buried her face in his chest, his flannel shirt bunching in her fingers. She whispered, "Your heart is pounding. It's all right now. It's all over."

He shook his head, jaw clenched, eyes closed. "The bastard is going to freeze to death out there." He stepped away, pulled on his boots, grabbed his coat, jammed his hands into gloves, and pulled his hat on his head.

Stella clung to him again. "You don't owe him anything! Don't go out there!"

He leaned down and kissed her, setting his palms on her cheeks. "I'm not doing it for him. I'm doing it for myself. I can't let myself become a monster that would let someone else, no matter how low, die."

"Come back to me." Stella rose on tiptoe to kiss him once more, snatching his breath away.

He pulled her into a fierce hug. "I will. Go sit by the wood stove and get warm."

Hours that seemed like days later, he returned with the coming of dawn. His hat, hair, and coat were dusted with snow, teeth chattering, as he burst through the door. Stella rushed to his side and helped him to peel off all his wet clothing and boots. He willingly let her lead him to a pile of blankets on the floor. She hurried to bring him hot tea that had been brewing on the wood stove, holding his hands as they trembled.

He nodded to her, his breath spilling out slowly. "Ah. That feels so good." She wrapped an arm around him, looking up at him expectantly. "He's in jail. A sheriff was waiting for him at the bottom of the trail. It turns out he's wanted for murder. He killed an old man who tried to stop him during a break-in. John Collins is finally going away for good." Jesse shuddered as silent tears slid down his face.

Stella pulled him close, stroking his head. "It's all right now. You're all right."

The next day, they made the trek into town, side by side. Stella held his hand as he sat in the office of the town store and pressed the phone to his ear. When his mother answered, he had to fight to keep himself from breaking down. "You don't have to hide anymore, Mama. It's all over. The monster is in jail. He will be for the rest of his days. It's over. It's finally over."

Chapter Thirteen

Stella stood at her front window, staring outside at the pine tree lit with sparkling lights as the snow drifted through the air. Christmas music played softly in the kitchen. Usually, it filled her with joy, but right now her heart was heavy. It lightened as a familiar figure approached from a distance. Snowshoes eased Jesse's travels, helping him to move quickly. He glanced at her window and a smile lit up his face.

Another bloomed on hers in answer, even as her eyes stung.

She lifted a hand to wave, keeping her eyes fixed on him until his footsteps thumped on her stairs and the door opened, bringing a breath of winter with him as a frigid breeze came with him, along with a burst of snow. "Brr! It's freezing out there today!" He stomped his feet on the mat and pulled off his boots. He hung his coat on the rack by the door. "You'll have to bundle up to your ears if you plan on going out. Might be best if we stay here, nice and cozy. No other place would be better." Happiness radiated from him, like a rainbow stretching across the sky after the rain had passed. He stepped forward and took her in his arms, kissing her until they were breathless and giggling. He grinned. "Sorry.

I just feel like I've been born again and started a new life." He glanced down and his smile slipped away. Her suitcase waited beside her, her coat folded over the top. Her boots were on her feet. The sparkle faded from his eyes.

"Oh, please don't look like that." Stella gripped his shoulders and gave him a little shake. "Please! It's not what you think!"

He pulled away and turned to the window. Staring at the glistening pine tree, his voice was flat. "You're leaving."

His pain was a punch to her stomach. It would have doubled her over if she didn't go to him and hold on to his back. "You know I have to go back to the city to turn in my story with my publisher and do my radio show. It's the reason I came here. I never expected I'd fall in love."

A quiver ran through him. Like he was barely holding it together before unraveling at the seams. He turned around and set his palm on her cheek, his thumb gently rubbing her jawbone. "I didn't expect it either…didn't know I even could…but I have fallen. So hard there's no coming back." He scraped at his face with one hand, cleared his throat, and pasted on a smile. "I'll walk with you to your car."

He picked up her coat and held it for her, allowing her to slip her arms inside, buttoning her up like she was a child. Or someone extremely cherished. They both stepped outside and strapped on their snowshoes. Jesse took her hand and gave it a squeeze. She took a few steps, stopped, and turned to look back at her pine tree. "I…I didn't turn off the radio."

"Don't worry. I'll come back and make sure everything is locked up." He wrapped an arm around her, and they continued down the mountain. It was the shortest journey she'd ever taken, time flying by with every step. The tiny cabin pulled at her heart—

—almost as fiercely as the man at her side.

At the trailhead, he gripped her shoulders and gave her a desperate kiss. When he pulled away, his voice was tortured. "I can't go with you. You mean everything to me, but I'm too broken. I can't face the city. I can't leave this place, and I don't blame you if you run as fast as you can and never look back."

She squeezed his hands. Hard. "You are *not* broken. You have put yourself back together." She tried to keep her voice from trembling. "I'm not running away. I just have to take care of my obligations. I have too many people I can't let down."

"Why does this feel like goodbye?" He held on tight.

"My mother always said it's 'see you soon.' Never goodbye. No matter how long it is."

He put her bag in the car and opened her door. He waited for the engine to fire up and poked her snowshoes in a snowbank. When her windows had defrosted and the heat flooded out the door, he bent down, threading his fingers in her hair, and kissed her until her insides melted. She closed her eyes, sighing softly. He whispered, "Drive safe." He stood back then ran alongside her as she pulled out, shouting loud enough to reach her through her windows and the loud blowing of the defrost fan. "Stella, I love you!"

She could barely see, her eyes watering so hard as she rolled down the window and blew him a kiss. "I love you more." He was the last thing she saw in the rearview mirror as she drove away.

When he was out of sight, she pulled over and cried her eyes out.

The four-hour drive went by in a blur. Stella honestly didn't even remember how she got to Broadway and the parking garage designated for her apartment building. She couldn't name a single Christmas song that had piped through her stereo for the entire drive. The city, all decked out for her favorite holiday, usually sent a thrill through her, making her feel alive. It did nothing when all she could think of was a little cabin in the woods—

—and the man inside it.

She went through the motions of unpacking her bag, throwing clothes in the washer, plugging in her laptop and sending her completed manuscript to her editor, publisher, and best friend. Standing at the window, a blinking sea of lights spread out before her as snow swirled in the air. None of it could touch the beauty of Stoner's Mountain. The alarm on her phone jarred her from the inner landscape of her mind and memories. Prompting her to change into fresh clothes, run a comb through her hair, and pull on her coat, a stylish coat, good enough to stand up to a less severe drop in temperature. The boots that carried her up the mountain on that first day, sliding and stumbling all the way, were good enough to navigate the hallway, elevator, and sidewalk running along the busy street. People jostled against her, pulling her along with the current of desperate shoppers trying to check off the rest of their to-do list for Christmas only two days away. She let them pull her along until a well-known sign appeared as if out of nowhere.

She broke away and walked through the doorway, a bell ringing overhead. *The Brew Factory* was in full swing, bustling with customers drinking some of their signature coffees and teas or indulging in refreshments straight out of a fairytale. Usually, the first whiff of pastries combined with coffee would propel Stella to heaven. Today, she didn't even notice.

"Stell! Over here!" Angie waved enthusiastically and jumped to her feet. "I've saved us a booth! Hurry! People are starting to grumble. We don't want it to get nasty in here so close to Christmas." She glared at the customers eyeing her table. "None of *you* want to be on the naughty list, do you?"

Stella couldn't hold back a giggle as she hurried across the room to save her friend from the mob. She flung her arms around Angie and rocked from side to side. "You look beautiful in that red sweater and beret with a white scarf. You're like a Christmas card."

"Sit." Her best friend patted the seat next to her even as she slid over. She tilted her head to study Stella more closely and bit her lip. "Now you, my friend, the girl who always acts like a Christmas fairy, swept away by the spirit of the season, you look like someone stole your dog, robbed your apartment, and popped your tires." She leaned in. "Missing your Mountain Man?" Stella couldn't even answer. She could only nod as she stared down at the tablecloth. Angie patted her hand. "I've already taken the liberty of ordering your favorite tea and scones…and here they are. They have magical powers. Let them cast a spell on you."

"Thank you, sweetheart. You're too good to me." She took a sip, and the delicious heat traveled to her shell-shocked heart. A bite of scone untied the knot in the pit of her stomach. She finished off the pastry and gave her friend another hug. "Much better."

Angie's smile was contagious. "Told you, darling, works like a charm, every time."

"I think the company has more to do with it." Stella sipped at her tea, and some of the pain weighing on her since the trek down the mountain eased. *You may have left a piece of your heart behind but it's not forever.*

Angie's arm wrapped around her waist. "You're sure about this, honey?"

Stella propped her head on her friend's shoulder, grateful it was strong and sturdy enough to carry both their troubles all these years. "I've never been more certain of anything in my entire life."

Jesse sat by his window, gazing into the night, marveling at the way the snow glistened in the moonlight, the dance of light and shadows. Hardly breathing, waiting with expectancy, he didn't understand why, not when Christmas Eve had never mattered to him. Nat King Cole's "The Christmas Song," brought a flash of memory, swaying in the kitchen with his mother as they baked cookies, until the voice of a radio broadcaster snapped him back to the present.

"Listeners, we have a special treat for you this evening. Stella Blair is here in the studio to read a selection from her latest Christmas story, just to give you a taste. Please welcome one of our favorite authors at the top the New York Times' Bestsellers list. You could not find a finer guest on Christmas Eve. I wish you could see her, everyone, in a green dress that glitters and dangling gold earrings flashing in the light. She's like a Christmas tree."

"Thank you so much, Brad. I'm so happy to be here on this holiest of nights. It's like the whole world is holding its breath, isn't it?" Jesse stood up and walked to his wood stove, staring into the flames, even as his whole body went tight at the sound of her voice. She laughed softly, a sound more beautiful than any music ever could be. "This is from *An Angel in the Wilderness.* I hope you enjoy listening as much as I loved writing it."

Jesse moved to the kitchen sink, gripping the edge with both hands, head bowed. Grappling with the fierce ache growing inside of him, he imagined this was how an amputee felt, longing for a missing limb. He closed his eyes and pictured her as she painted the picture of a rugged, bearded, tormented mountain man, someone Jesse might see looking in the mirror. A man who carried a lovely lost traveler through a blizzard, to his cabin, and made his way into her heart.

At the end of the broadcast, her boyfriend from the city found her, but she stood at the door and wouldn't let him in. "I'm sorry, John. I'm not the girl for you." Stella took a deep breath, tugging at Jesse's heart and went on. "The man she was supposed to spend the rest of her life with in only a few more hours hugged her and stared into her eyes. 'I know. I've known it for a long time. I'm not the one for you either. Take care of yourself, Misty.' He walked out of the room, past the Mountain Man, who stepped forward and took her hands, hope burning brightly in his eyes. '*Really*? You're staying here? With me?' She stepped into his arms, pressed her head to his chest. 'Yes. Yes. I couldn't go anywhere else. You're my angel in the wilderness.'"

Jesse turned off the radio, twisting the knob so hard he was surprised it didn't snap off. He scraped at his cheeks with his sleeve, shoulders hunched, wishing more than anything that real life could mirror that fairytale. The tears came anyway. He covered his face with his hands and let the misery have him. "God, how I wish she was here."

The door burst open. Heart pounding, he spun around, fists raised—

—expecting his father.

Stella stepped in. Her cheeks were rosy from the trek up the mountain. "Sometimes wishes do come true." Her hair whipped around her with the wind. Snow dusted her hat and her lashes. She ran across the room and flung her arms around him. "Did you really think I could leave you?"

"*How*?" He took her face in both his hands, drinking her in. "How can you be here? You were just on the radio in New York City."

"We taped the radio show this morning, and I drove back here without stopping, to get back to you." Her eyes filled and the tears spilled down her cheeks, "I never left, not really. My heart was here with you. Always with you."

He held her close, eyes going wide. "My God, you're shaking! You must be freezing! It's got to be about zero out there. What were you thinking?

She wrapped her arms around his neck. "About writing *our* next chapter. Right here."

"This is going to be enough for you? You're used to so much more." He peeled off her coat, pulled off her boots, and carried her to the rug in front of the wood stove.

She wrapped her arms around him. "All I need is you. Where I am and all the extras aren't important. So, what do you say?"

"Start writing…after we kiss."

They stayed up late into the night watching the snow falling, the piles mounting higher and higher. And still found themselves side by side come Christmas morning.

Epilogue

"*Angel in the Wilderness* skyrocketed straight to the top of the New York Times' bestseller list in only a week while it peaked on Amazon before it was even released. Stella Blair's journey into the Adirondacks of Upstate New York has carried her readers along with her. Eager to devour more, bombarding her with requests for more. But before another novel, a movie is in the making this summer. Bravo, Miss Blair. You've become America's favorite author!" Jesse tapped her picture taking up a full page of *The New Yorker*, his gaze traveling over her from head to toe. "This picture is beautiful, but it can't shine a candle on the day you came here wobbling on your high heeled boots and covered with snow from head to toe."

Stella shook a finger at him even as she pressed herself closer to his side. "You can just wipe that grin from your face, mister. Making fun of your bride to be the night before her wedding isn't right."

He set the magazine aside and rolled over to cover her in kisses. "I'm just having a little fun. You know it. I'm so proud of you and all your accomplishments."

"My greatest accomplishment is you." She lost herself in his eyes, something that wasn't hard to do, shaking herself out of a daze as his hand stroked her cheek. "I don't know how I'll make it to the morning."

Jesse pulled her close. "I can stay here to help you pass the time. We can suffer together." He winked. "I'm just as anxious as you. Afraid you'll come to your senses and run away in the night."

She rose up on her elbows. "Now, Jesse Collins, that is quite enough. I came to my senses the day I fell in love with you. And I'm sorry, but you can't stay. You're not supposed to see me until the wedding."

Jesse sighed heavily. "Well, I'd best be heading home now. It's late. Wouldn't want to be attacked by a bear."

Stella accompanied him to the door of her cabin. She extended her stay for several months—until she was ready to make the move into her new permanent home. A tiny cabin that was better than any palace as far as she was concerned. She buttoned Jesse's jacket and held out his gloves and hat. She rose on tiptoe to kiss him one more time. "Be careful going home. Tomorrow can't come fast enough. Becoming your wife is better than all my Christmases and birthdays in my life!"

He hugged her close, burying his face in her hair. "You are my everything." He opened the door and stepped out, calling back to her, "I love you."

"I love you more." Stella waved to him from the open doorway until he was no longer in sight. She sat by her window, watching the snow fall, unable to sleep, waiting for morning to come. With the first rays of sunlight, she couldn't help calling out her window, "Happy Valentine's Day! Today is my wedding day!" She dashed out in the snow and spun in circles, heart light, laughter bubbling over. *It's the happiest day of my life, Mama!* A cardinal dressed in brilliant red feathers landed on her illuminated pine.

Proving Mama was with her on this unforgettable day.

"Do you, Jesse Collins, take Stella Blair to be your wife, to have and to hold, in sickness and in health, 'til death do you part?" The pastor waited expectantly for his answer.

A shudder ran through him, but he forced it down and stared into the most beautiful eyes he'd ever seen. "I do."

"Do you, Stella Blair, take Jesse Collins to be your husband, to have and to hold, in sickness and in health, 'til death do you part?" A smile tugged at the elderly pastor's lip.

Stella nodded. "I do. Death won't be able to touch us. Nothing will."

The pastor raised his hands above their heads. "By the power invested in me by the church and the state of New York, I now pronounce you husband and wife. You may kiss the bride."

The applause was thunderous, so loud, it left Jesse's ears ringing. It didn't matter. Staring at his new wife and rolling *Mrs. Stella Collins* over and over in his mind was music—the most beautiful song he'd ever hear. Her eyes sparkled as she whispered, "Aren't you going to kiss me?"

She didn't need to ask him twice, one arm wrapping around her waist, the other cradling the back of her head. He pressed his lips to hers, and it was like they'd never kissed before. Fireworks burst in his mind. The earth shook beneath his feet. Everyone, and everything, in the small church went away—

—except her.

Loud music piped from the organ and cheers echoed around them. He opened his eyes. Stella looked as starstruck as he felt. "Can we stand here forever?"

He chuckled and swept a hand in the air to encompass the crowd. "I think they're waiting for us."

Smiles beamed. Cameras flashed as everyone captured the moment. Jesse tucked his new wife's arm in his and towed her to the front to receive their guests. He had no one in attendance. His childhood years didn't leave any doors open for friendship. He couldn't talk about life at home, nor could anyone ever come to his house. Stella's abundance of family, friends, and close acquaintances made up for it, as they opened their arms and hearts for him.

Finally, the two stood alone at the entrance of the church, white lights strung overhead like twinkling stars. The others had gone on to the only restaurant in town that would host their reception, open to guests and any locals who wished to celebrate with them. Jesse took Stella in his arms. "Dance with me?"

She nodded and they swayed gently round and round until his back was turned to the nave of the church. Her feet went still. She squeezed his shoulders, leaned in close, and spoke softly in his ear, "Jesse...turn around."

Slowly, he did as she asked. And the world stopped spinning. His breath caught in his chest. His heart raced like a bird madly fluttering its wings, battering against a window when trapped in the house. His line of sight narrowed, homing in on a woman in a simple dress of pale blue. Her dark hair was cut in a bob, curling around her jaw, her bangs drifting over eyes blazing like blue fire. Somehow, she seemed much smaller than ever before. "Mom?" His voice cracked.

She stepped forward and flung her arms around him. "Oh Jesse. All this time, it's like I've been shipwrecked on an abandoned island without you."

"And I've been stranded here on Stoner's Mountain." He didn't even fight the tears spilling over as he kissed her cheek and held her tight. "How? How did you get here?"

Laura Collins reached out her hand, drawing Stella into their circle. "A special someone made it happen."

Jesse's heart nearly burst. He kissed Stella on the crown of her head. "Thank you. This means the world to me." He wrapped an arm around her shoulders, turning her toward the other most important woman in his life. "Mom, I'd like you to meet my bride, Stella Blair."

Stella's laugh was a song. "That's Stella Collins. Welcome home, Mrs. Collins."

As Jesse held on to the two people who meant more to him than life itself, he realized, for the first time, he was home.

Her name was Stella.

Author's Note

A shout out to Michael Hardy for lighting the flames of inspiration with "Wait in the Truck."

To Nicholas Stoner, a man who epitomized starting over—again and again—a teen in the American Revolution who fought—fought valiantly—with Benedict Arnold before he was a turncoat, accompanied John Andre, spy, to the gallows, and made it to Yorktown for England's surrender. He joined the fight yet again in the War of 1812. A true patriot. Husband to a war widow and father to a daughter who was not his own. Deputy sheriff. Hunter, trapper, guide in the Adirondacks. A mountain could only be named after an American hero who scaled one challenge after another and never backed down.

Heidi Sprouse lives in upstate NY in historic Johnstown. She attended college at St. Rose in Albany, knowing all along her two loves were teaching and English. It took four years before she landed the teaching job of her dreams, but over twenty years later she is still nurturing young minds. She loves the privilege of watching practically-new little humans as they discover and begin to shape their own worlds.

Knowing what she wants and going after it in relentless pursuit is Sprouse's gift. Deciding to become an author can be downright unnerving, but Sprouse bit into the challenge, took off, and never looked back. Her perseverance proves success is not a matter of luck. It's a matter of finding what speaks to your heart and committing to do that thing until it makes a difference.

When she isn't busy teaching or with her husband Jim, her son Patrick, her daughter in law Cheyenee, and her canine kids Remington and Ruger, she's cooking up her next novel. She dabbles in sweet romances, historical fiction, and suspense thrillers, depending on what pleases her reader's eye at any given moment. Sprouse is always in search of the extraordinary in the ordinary, writing about strong men with old-fashioned values and the women who pick them up when they fall. She'll tell anyone it's never too late to chase after your dreams, no dream is too small or insignificant, and any mountain can be moved with a proposal and a good plan.

Her past works include: *All the Little Things, Lightning Can Strike Twice, Aging Gracefully, Sunny Side Up, Against the Grain, Hope's Rise From Ashes, When You Wish Upon a Christmas Tree, Adirondack Sundown, The Edge of Forgiveness on Blue Mountain, Sunrise Over Indian Lake, Deserted on Lake Desolation, One Last Adirondack Summer, Whispers of Liberty, Liberty's Promise, Liberty's Legacy, Rosie and her Ragamuffin Sam, Mouse, Lion, Walking with Ghosts on Ward's Pond, Our Hearts are Blind,* and others. Stay tuned for more to come!

www.ingramcontent.com/pod-product-compliance
Lightning Source LLC
Chambersburg PA
CBHW010600310726
48969CB00009B/2506